SHERLOCK HOLMES AND THE HOLBORN EMPORIUM

In High Holborn, quite close to Hatton Garden, stands the famous emporium of A. W. Forrage Ltd. Everything in this amazing Edwardian department store should have run like clockwork, but unfortunately there was sabotage afoot. Nasty accidents started to happen and, fearful of closure, the management sought out the assistance of Sherlock Holmes and Dr Watson. But who was determined to destroy a London landmark? And what was the fiendish saboteur's motive?

Books by Val Andrews
in the Linford Mystery Library:

VAL ANDREWS

◆

SHERLOCK HOLMES AND THE HOLBORN EMPORIUM

Complete and Unabridged

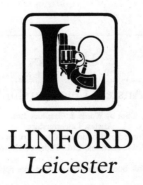

LINFORD
Leicester

First published in Great Britain in 2001 by
Breese Books Limited, London

First Linford Edition
published 2003
by arrangement with
Breese Books Limited, London

British Library CIP Data

Andrews, Val
  Sherlock Holmes and the Holborn Emporium
  Large print ed.—
  Linford mystery library
  1. Holmes, Sherlock (Fictitious character)
  —Fiction 2. Watson, John H. (Fictitious
  character)—Fiction 3. Private investigators
  —England— London—Fiction
  4. Detective and mystery stories
  5. Large type books
  I. Title
  823.9'14 [F]

  ISBN 1–8439–5010–3

Published by
F. A. Thorpe (Publishing)
Anstey, Leicestershire

Printed and bound in Great Britain by
T. J. International Ltd., Padstow, Cornwall

Introduction

In High Holborn, quite close to Hatton Garden, stands that wondrous emporium of A. W. Forrage Ltd. A huge overgrown drapers originally, the store has grown through the years so that each and every one of its many departments upon its several floors has grown to be famous in its own right. It has been said that you can buy anything at 'Forrage's', from a thimble to an elephant! Although this may no longer be quite true at the time of writing 'Forrage's of Holborn' still flourishes, yet may never again quite capture its halcyon days when the twentieth century was still very young and Sherlock Holmes was still at 221B Baker Street.

Indeed it was towards the end of 1903 that my friend became involved with the famous store. In fact I speak of one of the last really noteworthy cases with which Sherlock Holmes concerned himself, prior to his retirement to keep bees upon

1

the Sussex Downs.

To this day, whenever I pass the now rather old fashioned department store with its silver recessed letters proclaiming 'A. W. Forrage' I remember the particular enterprise in which we became engaged. Those of you who remember the store at its height will enjoy being reminded of what a pleasure it was to take a 'Forage around Forrage's'. Others will perhaps enjoy reading something of the store that was so much a part of the London scene, especially at the festive season. Yes, everyone went to Forrage's at Christmas where everything they could possibly desire appeared to be for sale. So let me take you back to an era when the big store and the great detective were both still in their prime.

John H. Watson
Finchley, December 1923

1

1

An Early Start

On a morning late in the November of 1903, I created something of a record at 221B Baker Street by turning up early at the breakfast table. My friend Sherlock Holmes was evidently indulging himself in a very rare lie-in. I tried to abandon my smug feelings as I raised the lid from a dish in order to spoon some kedgeree onto my plate. But as I did so I noticed an envelope lying upon that platter. It had my name written upon it but there was no address and no stamp. My name had been written in Holmes's unmistakable hand, but if he had something to tell me why did he not at least extend his head around my bedroom door in order to do so? I opened the envelope, unfolded the sheet of paper which I took from within and read:

221B Baker Street. 9 a.m.

My dear Watson,

Whilst you were still in the arms of Morpheus I received a message to the effect that I should meet a client in Holborn. I suggest that when you have breakfasted you meet me in the restaurant at Forrage's where we can partake of luncheon. May I suggest twelve-noon?

Yours sincerely,
Sherlock Holmes

I ignored his irony and decided to take him up on his invitation. In any case it had been an age since I had visited Forrage's so I decided to go there at once in order to give myself a chance to tour a place long remembered with affection; the Christmas season was practically upon us which would, I felt, add much to the enjoyment of such an expedition. As a boy I had visited Santa Claus there in his grotto, and as a student I had purchased necessities of an academic and medical life at Forrage's. More recently I had obtained a cabin trunk there prior to my expedition to Afghanistan, and a few years back I had bought bargain clothing in a Forrage's sale, at a time when I had depended on a meagre army pension. But I had not crossed its friendly portals since the turn of the century; a situation that I anticipated putting to rights with pleasure.

* * *

From the opposite side of High Holborn to that upon which stood the world-famous emporium, I took in the brightly lit, enticing vista which was presented by Forrage's display windows, prior to crossing for a closer inspection. At the Leather Lane end I saw first the ladies' fashions displayed upon manikins which have since all but disappeared. Their wigs, false lashes and brows give them a rather charmingly eerie appearance; rather like rejected models from Madame Tussaud! They stood, sat or leaned in their series of skirts, dresses and blouses. The next window featured men's suitings, which I felt in a more sound position to criticise. It is a sign of advancing age, dear reader, when you look into a shop window and shudder at the sight of fashions which appal you, along with horrendous accessories such as boots with pointed toes and shirts with their collars permanently attached.

More show windows followed an entrance, each with its individual example of the scene painter's art as backing. For example, the children's toys were displayed upon papier mâché rocks, before a backdrop depicting the inside of a cave. There were stuffed animals of great realism, as if brought straight from Regent's Park, and mechanical marvels of engineering and clockwork. In other words there was not a Noah's Ark, Dutch doll, Jack-in-the-box or monkey on a stick to be seen.

The music window was likewise without the wonders of my youth. Gone were the pianola rolls and music boxes, but well displayed was a contraption titled 'The Grama-Forrage', featuring flat discs rather than the earlier cylinders.

However, there were violins, guitars and flutes, tastefully arranged around a grand piano. Bull pups and tiny spaniels cavorted in the pet department window, part of which had been transformed into a giant aquarium, so that one could see the golden orfe and such varieties actually swimming immediately behind the window glass itself. Another entrance, then beyond that the window display of the conjuring department with a display of mysterious-looking cones, cans and caddies all enamelled with cabalistic signs and the like. More impressive impedimenta of illusion included a satyr's head with a mouth which opened and closed at intervals to reveal a playing card upon its tongue, and a large all-glass casket filled with conjurer's paper flowers. A placard assured us that 'A professional conjurer is present at all times to demonstrate 'Forrage's Magic'.' Finally a window filled with bicycles, tandems, tricycles and even a motorised bicycle. All were arranged before an actual motor car in which sat a moustached and begoggled dummy, reminiscent of the famous music hall comedian, Harry Tate!

Did I say 'finally'? Well, I remember now that I have neglected to mention windows full of mouth-watering comestibles and sweetmeats and bottles of wine displayed in a party setting with lots of streamers and confetti about.

As if all this were not enough to tempt the bypasser to enter and 'Forage a while' there was a placard which announced that in the basement could be seen a 'Complete Circus' which included a live elephant with performances 'thrice daily'. Also of course, Santa Claus could be visited in his grotto 'At the earth's core', the cost of the trip being threepence for all persons, this price including a present for each and every child.

Suddenly I realised that I had been slowly getting cold as I surveyed these windows. The entrance doors to the great big store were enticing, so I walked through into the warmth and wonders of Forrage's.

It was only ten o'clock, I had two hours to explore the wonders within and wasted not a second of that time. Yet by the time

I had seen the demonstration of golf clubs by 'a well known professional' who entreated everyone to 'keep an eye on the ball' and the practicalities of a patent ice cream maker, it was all but eleven, and there was so much to crowd into just one hour. For example, who could resist the chance to fondle a real live tiger cub in the pets department? A small boy in a silk hat and Eton suit screwed a monocle into his left eye and announced, 'Bai Jove, pater, I weally would like this fella for me Cwistmas box, what?'

A faultlessly attired gentleman with a velvet-trimmed collar to his greatcoat replied, 'Weally, Weggie, I think a wabbit might be more pwactical!'

The young swell looked as if he usually got what he wanted, so I pitied the poor tiger cub, hoping it would not finish up roaring with an aristocratic lisp.

I visited one or two more departments, but only with the swiftness of an American visiting the British Museum, for it was all but time for me to keep my appointment with Sherlock Holmes.

My friend was seated with a menu in

his left hand. With his right he appeared to be conducting the three-piece miniature orchestra upon the dais.

'My dear Watson, what will you have? I am all for a plate of gammon and spinach.'

I chose the roast beef and we shared a bottle of hock. It was hardly the right beverage to go with the beef, but its lightness recommended it, for I suspected that we might need clear heads later. Holmes explained, 'A. W. Forrage wishes to see us in his office on the top floor at one, Watson, but we still have good time to consume our meal and observe that which we see about us. What do you make of the incomplete quartette?'

I answered his question with another. 'Not a trio, as it appears to be?'

'No, Watson, the arrangements which are being played have been scored for a quartette. If you listen carefully you will detect that there are certain passages where a harp should be involved. Moreover, if you observe carefully you will see the shape of a harp, draped with a blanket, behind the piano.'

10

A glance was enough to confirm his statement and I looked at the menu for more information. Confidently I said, 'The Signor Pescalini Quartette: well, at least I can see that he is Italian.'

I had referred to the fiercely waxed moustache and clearly defined black side burns, arranged like twin curls. Holmes chuckled, 'An Italian from Killarney, Watson.'

'What makes you say that?'

'To begin with, that he is Irish is suggested by certain ethnic characteristics. If you look carefully you will see that his black hair is red at its roots, and blue eyes, large ears and pointed nose are all Irish characteristics.'

'Do they suggest Killarney?'

My question was ironic but his answer was not. 'Notice, Watson, the way he holds his violin with its neck turned towards his audience. He holds and bows it more like a gypsy fiddler than an Italian maestro. A fiddler with a style suggestive of the Killarney tinkers.'

I was not completely convinced until the violinist-leader signalled to his pianist and celloist to cease, and then spoke with an Italian accent that could well have been assumed. 'Ladies and gentlemen, is there anything you would like to hear?'

There followed one of those dreadful silences so often produced by an English crowd, even in the metropolis. Then Sherlock Holmes spoke up with a clear, loud voice. 'How about Killarney?'

At first the Signor started, then grinned broadly and started to play of Killarney's lakes and fells, in a manner wild, which his colleagues could not follow. As we applauded, Holmes smiled in triumph.

★ ★ ★

It was at exactly five minutes before one o'clock that we reached the top floor by means of one of the lifts, operated by an old soldier minus his right arm. Fortunately he needed only his left to operate the lever on the half wheel which indicated the floor required. His throwing of another lever started what was to me a perilous means of ascension.

'A.W.' himself proved to be a rather

fearsome-looking old gentleman, clad in a frock coat of a kind which I remembered being worn by floorwalkers in the days of my youth.

'Mr Holmes, I was not expecting you to be accompanied; my business with you is strictly confidential.'

Holmes put a great deal of meaning into his pronunciation of his few words of reply. 'As is my friend and colleague, Dr John H. Watson.'

Forrage inclined his head slightly. 'Obviously I must accept someone in whom you yourself have trust. How do you do, Dr Watson.'

The department store 'king' bowed us into 'thrones' only slightly less opulent than his own. As I seated myself I glanced round, and noticed what a splendidly appointed office it was, with a wide span of window which gave a breathtaking view of the dome of St Paul's. 'A.W.'s' gold-rimmed pince-nez and bejewelled watch chain which spanned his bulging waistcoat added to this setting for a wildly successful store owner. He brushed his grizzled moustaches with the fingers of his right hand and said, 'I will not beat around the bush, gentlemen; I am not, despite my wealth, a spendthrift. These trappings of opulence which you see about you were not obtained through a personal desire for luxury. Rather they are part of my stock in trade, necessary to impress, but for business reasons only. Like my many departments, my Christmas grotto and the circus in my basement, they cost a fortune but help me to make an even bigger one. But then this, Mr Detective, you will have realised. Can you deduce anything else about me?'

Holmes obviously realised that he was being given some sort of test; one to which he was of course more than equal. He said, 'I perceive, Mr Forrage, that you buy only the best but make sure that you get your value from it. You have an eye upon fashion where the cost can be controlled, you suffer from indigestion, gout and with your liver. You have many enemies.'

Forrage raised an admonishing hand. 'Stop! You sound like the palmist in the ground-floor tea lounge. Yes, I will pay the price for what I want but I expect quality and long usage.'

Holmes smiled. 'Modern office furnishings would need frequent replacement if they were not to appear *passé*; but genuine antiques keep their fashion and their value. Your clothing is also expensive, but tailored to last. When you had your breeches let out at the waist you also had permanent turn-ups added to them. So you have an eye for fashion.'

Forrage looked a trifle embarrassed. 'How could you possibly know that I had my trousers let out at the waist, or that they were not tailored with turn-ups to start with?'

'Mr Forrage, you cannot disguise the fact that the creases in your trousers have changed their position. This makes the alteration as obvious to me as it would be had I seen the gusset hidden by your coat tails. As for the turn-ups; this fashion was started by His Majesty King Edward, but he was still Prince of Wales at the time, and your trousers are probably seven or eight years old?'

Forrage nodded dumbly and then

asked wearily, 'I suppose the problems with my general health are just as obvious to you?'

Holmes replied, 'That you are a hearty trencherman is obvious from the fact that your breeches have had to be enlarged. A vast intake of food usually leads to indigestion. Your high colour suggests a similar liking for wines and spirits, which in turn will usually result eventually in gout and liver problems. I feel sure that Dr Watson will bear out my words?'

I nodded and said, 'Quite so.'

'A.W.' relaxed his features into a wide grin of resignation. 'Holmes, you are honest as well as all but frighteningly observant. You were right about the enemies too.'

Holmes nodded. 'Of course, no man can rise to such giddy heights as you have, sir, without upsetting many rivals and envious persons. Come, have I passed your test?'

'You beat me at my own game. Let us get down to business. I am being blackmailed.'

Holmes nodded as if he had guessed as

much. 'By whom, and why do you not call in the police?'

Forrage was no longer relaxed. 'If I knew who was blackmailing me I would be engaged at this moment in breaking his neck rather than consulting a detective. As for the police, why they would be all over my beautiful store in their great hob-nailed boots, frightening children in the grotto, ladies in the fashion department, and attracting the attention of journalists who would bankrupt me if they got a whisper and made it public.'

Holmes took a proferred cigar from a silver box but waved aside the silver-mounted lighter and lit it with a vesta. I refused the offered cigar and lit an Egyptian cigarette.

'It started, Mr Holmes, with a note, typed with one of those infernal machines, doubtless so as not to leave any handwriting clue. I sell those wretched typewriters, but always did think they would cause trouble of various kinds. The message was to the effect that I was to pay a large sum in order to avoid my groceries being interfered with!'

'What was your reaction to this demand?'

'Well, not to pay it, I assure you. I just doubled all precautions with the groceries.'

'Did anything untoward occur?'

'We discovered tintacks mixed with the currants. Very hard to spot, but the member of my staff who was weighing up half a pound realised how few of them seemed to supply that weight. We were able to dispose of the whole batch of currants before any of them had been sold. Of course the fiend who put the tacks in the currants could still be unaware that they were discovered.'

'Has any subsequent threat been received?'

'I'm coming to that ... a few days ago I received another typed message threatening to interfere with articles in my cosmetic department. Again we thwarted the blighter by discovering caustic soda in a consignment of bath salts. But now, only hours ago, I received yet another note, typed as were the others, threatening that something might happen to children visiting Santa Claus in the grotto.'

A look of despair had almost begun to cross his rubicund face as he thrust three neatly typewritten messages across the table that Holmes might inspect them. My friend studied them carefully in turn, using his lens. Then he pushed them across to me.

'Well, Watson, what do you make of them?'

I laid the three squares of paper side by side upon the table and studied them at length, saying, 'Identical pieces of paper folded neatly so that the corners exactly correspond. Your man is neat and precise. Apart from that, each of the messages was typed upon the same machine.'

'What makes you say that?'

'Why, Holmes, did you not yourself tell me that no two typewriters produce results that are exactly alike? I have read your monograph upon the subject and . . .'

My friend interrupted. 'You refer to slight imperfections in letters, slight lack of alignment and things of that sort. Where are the imperfections and eccentricities of alignment, or even change of density?'

I replied, 'There are no such imperfections at all . . . that is just it . . . they must therefore be produced on the same, rare, absolutely perfect typewriter.'

Holmes was at his most irritating as he said, 'Watson, you are jumping to a very interestingly incorrect conclusion. What you say about my own studies of the imperfection is true . . . but only where the machine has been in use for at least a few days. It is use itself which produces imperfection. These notes were each produced with a brand new Remington portable. In each case both the machine and the ribbon were brand new.'

'You mean with three different machines and three ribbons, never in use before?'

'At last, exactly, bravo!'

'But why would anyone do that?'

'So that we cannot trace him through his typewriter, or any other that he might use, assuming that he continues to follow this procedure.'

Chastened, I gave the matter thought before saying, 'So, we have a shrewd man, rather than some idiot playing practical jokes. He must be of some means if he buys a brand-new portable Remington every time he sends one of these messages. He must be demanding a very large sum.'

It was A. W. Forrage who replied, 'Dr Watson, two thousand pounds is not, to me, an enormous sum. But I have not dwelt seventy years upon this planet without learning that you can never, ever pay off a blackmailer. Once paid he will come back for more, again and again and again.'

Holmes nodded. 'I notice that he is not specific about his plans for the children in the grotto. I will undertake to investigate this matter but on one condition . . . that if at any point I decided that life and limb are actually endangered you will call in Scotland Yard?'

Grudgingly, Forrage nodded.

'For the moment, Watson and I will

wander down to Santa's grotto and see if we can discern anything of interest.'

Although his visage had threatened apoplexy at the mention of Scotland Yard, Forrage quickly calmed, saying, 'I realise that your hands are tied, as are mine, but if you can find a way of not involving the authorities, I will double your fee, whatever that may be!'

Holmes said, as I expected, 'I do not vary my charge, save where I omit it entirely. Dukes and dustmen, you know, they are all the same to me.'

Forrage grunted, 'Not a socialist by any chance are you?'

Holmes glared at the store magnate. 'No, sir, I am entirely without political affiliation, or even interest for that matter. I am fortunate in being able to write my own rules as well as follow them.'

2

The Grotto of Peril

Was 'Santa's Grotto' the invention of
A. W. Forrage? I don't know, but I
remember as a very small child being
taken to see Santa (or rather 'Father
Christmas' as we referred to him in those
days), in a local store where he had a
large sack of toys or sometimes a bran
tub. One just paid a penny and trotted off
happily enough with a small gift. Forrage
it probably was who made Santa into the
star of a sort of theatrical production.
Every year he changed the setting, from
Iceland to China or Aladdin's cave to Red
Riding Hood's wood. One might visit
'Wonderland' and be taken by Alice to the
tea party to meet the March Hare, the
Dormouse and the Mad Hatter. Some
years the children would be transported
to their imaginary destination in a
fanciful mode of transport: an airship to

the Alps or a mechanical sledge to Toyland. But for the Christmas season with which we were involved the theme was one of visiting the bowels of the earth, so we joined a party of Forrage patrons and their offspring, crowding into 'The Earth Skewer', which was one of Forrage's lifts, disguised to seem like a contraption dreamed up by H. G. Wells or Jules Verne. The lift entrance was decorated with papier mâché rocks and the door itself painted to seem like the entrance to a vehicle of the imagination. Beside it stood an elderly, out-of-work actor who recited, over and over again, 'This way to the centre of the earth to see Santa ... have your threepence ready, please!'

Inside the lift an operator dressed as an elf threw the lever and everyone gasped with amazed anticipation as red foil rattled upon the walls of the apartment as it descended very slowly to the floor below. The elf shouted as we barely moved ... 'Thirty thousand feet ... seventy thousand ... two hundred thousand ... one million feet into the earth's core!'

As the doors opened again we emerged into an obstacle course of plaster rockwork, imitation red cinders and a path which we followed as red lights flashed amid at least a shillings worth of artificial fog. These properties and effects gave a delicious series of evocative odours, size, glue, gunpowder, varnish and disinfectant.

At length we reached a cave, inside which sat Santa himself: a stout man in a red suit trimmed with white fur, and sporting a huge white hook-on beard. He guffawed and chuckled wearily, seating unwilling children upon his ample knee as he demanded to know what they would like for Christmas. He had a sense of humour too, asking a prosperous-looking eight-year-old what he would like. The child said, 'I want a bicycle.'

Santa chuckled and produced a small festively wrapped packet which he handed to the child, saying, 'Here is a nice puncture-mending outfit, just in case you get one!'

He gave a bar of soap to a boy with a dirty neck, and a little girl who demanded a doll's house of a certain style and colour was given a tiny replica of a house. He told her, 'That'll teach you not to specify too much!'

But I noticed that the quiet, pleasant children got quite impressive-looking toys. Holmes nodded his approval. 'Very shrewd, Watson. A perfect example of how to sell the unsaleable. Last year's remainders, soiled goods, left-overs. Better to get threepence for them than pay someone to take them away.'

Then quite suddenly the sounds of joy and pleasurable anticipation were surmounted by a series of dismayed shouts, surprise and even fear. Children were crying and their parents were shouting, angrily.

'Ooh, Mummy, what is it?'

'Shame!'

'Help, there is something horrid in my present!'

'Disgusting!'

'Where is Mr Forrage?'

I turned to my friend and said, 'Not all that shrewd after all, Holmes; the recipients are far from delighted.'

It appeared that only the last few packets that we had seen handed out contained the boxed spiders, dead mice, sneezing powder, evil-smelling liquids disguised as perfume, and chocolates filled with mustard rather than caramel. Santa was fierce in his protestations of innocence. Loudly he proclaimed that he had no control over the wrapped items. Holmes took the opportunity to nudge himself nearer to the large box from which the gifts were taken by Santa. After a quick look he turned to me and explained. 'There is a chute from above, Watson, down which someone drops the packages. Quick, follow me, and we will take the back stairs. We must try to find out from where they are dropped, and I fancy it may be some minutes before the lift resumes its transport of the public.'

We dashed up the stone steps, sometimes two at a time, and I was quite breathless when we reached the floor above. Sherlock Holmes, clearly in better physical condition than I, was scarcely out of breath, and using his instinct for position and distance he soon found the place from whence he believed the packages had been dropped. Pushing his way through a door marked 'Staff Only' he amazed those within by putting a stop to their activities of feeding packages into the chute.

'Stop! Where did you get this present batch of parcels?'

A bewildered youth replied, 'A boy brought them from the depository, in this box.'

The youth indicated a cardboard container. A girl asked, 'What is it to you . . . who do you think you are?'

This girl had recognised that we were not of her breed, nor yet of that which normally harangued her with orders. In the manner of most repressed persons she began to vent her repression upon those who held for her no fear. I tried to calm her. 'Dear lady, we have been asked to investigate a certain situation that is not any fault of your own.'

She retorted, 'Store detectives, eh . . . why didn't you say?'

But the youth was more co-operative and said, 'Come to think of it I didn't recognise the boy who brought this box, and it *is* different from the others.'

Holmes examined the box and opened one of the gaily wrapped packages within it. This contained what was supposed to be a box of fancy handkerchiefs but in fact contained a folded blood-stained cloth. He said, 'I will take the box, meanwhile I suggest that you examine one in four of the gifts before you feed them into the chute.'

We repaired to Forrage's office, where we found him just returned from one of his frequent forays around his store. We showed him the box and to our surprise he appeared to recognise it, saying, 'Why, that is the box that I saw the boy deliver to the room where the toy chute is housed.'

Holmes demanded, 'You saw a boy handling this box? What boy, who was he?'

Forrage replied, 'Mr Holmes, I have hundreds of employees. I cannot be expected to recognise every one of them, let alone remember their names. About twenty minutes ago I was on a regular tour of inspection. Passing the room where the toy chute is I saw that box being handed through the door by a boy of about fourteen years.'

I dared to ask, 'You cannot name your employee, yet you remember the appearance of an individual cardboard box?'

'In this case certainly, because I know that boxes of a certain design and colour are being employed to transport the wrapped toys from the depository. We have system here, Doctor, system.'

Holmes asked, 'You challenged this boy?'

'Certainly. I said, 'Look here, boy, what are you doing with that box? It is not your job to bring it here.' In return he was insolent so I asked him, 'What is your weekly wage?' He said, 'Fifteen bob!' So I took fifteen shillings from my pocket, gave it to him and said, 'Now get out, I never want to see you in my store again!' I paid him off, d'ye see?'

Despite his concern, Holmes chuckled and said, 'Yes, I do see: but Mr Forrage, if my deductions are correct this boy did not even work for you. He was probably the innocent messenger of your enemies. He was doubtless tipped to bring the box to the room where the chute is housed. I would not worry that you did not recognise him: he has little significance, being a mere pawn.'

But Forrage was furious, 'Not worry? Do you realise that I have allowed myself to be diddled out of fifteen shillings? He defrauded me by failing to mention that he was not a member of my staff when I handed him that money.'

I tried to calm him. 'Come, sir, no harm has been done, surely.'

He expostulated, 'No harm? It is I who have been done!'

'But it was only fifteen shillings.'

'A paltry sum, but I have built up this great store through shrewdness and good husbandry, not through being diddled by urchins.'

Holmes stifled a chuckle as he began to examine the box. At length he spoke seriously about that which he saw. 'Here, if I am not mistaken, we have a cardboard container of the style and colour used by the tradespeople of Clerkenwell Road. Off that thoroughfare lies a labyrinth of small mean streets where live and work many hundreds of immigrant workers. Many, a great many, of these are honest and diligent, yet some come from countries where large-scale extortion is the norm rather than the exception. There is nothing to give us a closer clue, save that I recognise it as being of a type and style used to pack wholesale quantities of tailoring accessories: buttons, spools of thread, waist buckles and the like. As for the packages within, they are somewhat roughly packed, covered in fancy paper of the type offered by street traders, not of the quality that one would expect at Forrage's. The string is of a kind that could be purchased almost anywhere and in itself tells us nothing; but the knots . . . what do you make of them, Watson?'

I looked at the knots carefully. 'They are roughly tied . . . '

'But firmly tied, Watson, these are no ordinary grannies or bows, these are seafarers' knots, half hitch, sheepshank and the like.'

I enquired, 'What will be your next move?'

'Oh, I will take the box back to Baker Street to study it further if I may?'

Forrage was calm now. 'Do with it what you will, but please do something about my problem.'

Holmes seemed a trifle more optimistic now. 'I will give it my urgent attention, but I would not worry too much. I imagine you have seen the last of your troubles in the grotto. Your enemy, or enemies, will now be considering the next move and which of your many departments he will give attention to next. So far these incidents, whilst irritating, have been of a comparatively harmless nature. We must act quickly, before they begin to be of a more serious nature. Fortunately he tends to warn you as to the direction of his attentions. But we cannot rely upon a continuance of this pattern.'

We took our leave of A. W. Forrage and a cab back to Baker Street. As we travelled, Holmes asked, 'Well, Watson, at least we were drawn in at the deep end very quickly, but what have we learned?'

I replied, with some confidence, 'The perpetrator could be an immigrant, residing or working in the Clerkenwell Road area. This person was possibly once a sailor and is not without means.'

'What makes you deduce that?'

'He has spent money upon a selection of gifts to adulterate, and papers and string with which to wrap them. He engaged a boy to deliver a box: oh, and there is the matter of three brand-new typewriters!'

'Excellent, Watson, we will make a detective of you yet! But seriously, an expense shared becomes much smaller.'

★　★　★

We spent an interesting hour opening and examining all of the remaining packages, and Mrs Hudson will, I feel sure, remember to this day the smells, shocks and minor explosions which occurred. I do believe that for a time the good lady believed us both to have quite lost our senses. However, when we explained to her in confidence the purpose of our experiments, her indignation took a different direction.

'Do you honestly mean to tell me, Mr Holmes, that some wicked fiend has tried to play such evil tricks upon little children and at Christmas time? I trust you will arrange some punishment that will make him laugh upon the other side of his face!'

Holmes smiled kindly at the dear soul and made no mockery of her honest concern. 'That I will, Mrs Hudson, but first I have to catch him.'

She threw up her hands with feeling, 'Oh, you'll do that, sir, you have never failed a soul in trouble yet.'

As she hurried away to go about her housekeeping duties, Sherlock Holmes was strangely softened from his usual style as he said to me, 'What a dear, kindly and long-suffering woman. Now, Watson, let us examine the remainder of these packets.'

There were more obnoxious smells and sensations, but as I remarked, they were all of a kind available from a dealer in practical joker's equipment.

However, Holmes said, 'Beware though, Watson, the practical joker who knows not where to stop.'

I asked, 'What shall you do if that happens?'

He replied, instantly, 'I will have no alternative but to inform Scotland Yard, even if Forrage does not like the idea. Speaking of Forrage, Watson, what do you make of him?'

I thought before I spoke, then said, 'I suppose one would have to call him the type of man who built the British Empire; but he built an empire of his own. He is, I consider, far seeing, a trifle humourless, enterprising to the extreme, loved yet feared by his employees, and perhaps a touch ruthless?'

Holmes nodded in agreement as he abandoned his delving into devilment and filled a calabash with Scottish mixture. When he had lit the pipe he leaned back in his chair and replied, 'My own feelings, Watson, and you were ever a good judge of human nature, even if you err upon the kindly side. A man does not reach Forrage's position without more than a hint of ruthlessness and had he believed that his paying two thousand pounds would have solved his problem he would have paid the blackmailer that sum. It is only his own shrewdness and the knowledge that it would not stop there that has made him involve me in his problems. Upon the morrow we will consult him again, and I fear that he will greet us with the news of another demand.'

This proved to be true, as we could read from the expression on Forrage's face when we next entered his grand apartment. That, and the neat white square of paper which lay upon his blotter. He greeted us with a hangdog air and once we had been seated he dispensed with other niceties, such as the handing out of cigars, and pushed the paper across the desk for our inspection. Holmes studied it carefully and then passed it to me. I saw that again the paper had been more than neatly folded and that the typing, typeface and ribbon were absolutely pristine. I read the terse message . . .

FORRAGE ... YOUR CONJURING DEPARTMENT WILL BE MYSTERIOUS INDEED IF YOU DO NOT LEAVE FIVE THOUSAND POUNDS WITH THE BLIND FLOWER SELLER.

Forrage explained, 'There is a blind woman who sells flowers from a pitch upon the opposite side of High Holborn.'

I nodded and said, 'I have noticed her. But I am extremely puzzled by the boldness of this suggestion. Surely he must know that it would be easy for you to watch for whoever collected the money from this woman?'

Holmes waved aside my remark. 'No, his plan is a good one, this woman does a thriving business, partly from the quality of her wares and partly through the inherent kindness of the public concerning her affliction. If you hand her an envelope, which she doubtless expects through prior consultation with our quarry, he would doubtless collect it from her when her trade is at its briskest. Perhaps this might occur at about four in the afternoon, when many shoppers are making their way to the underground railway.'

I could see his point; it would be impossible to follow a suspect where he could be one of dozens. I said without conviction, 'Maybe one of us could dress as a tramp and hang around the flower seller so that we could actually see an envelope change hands. Then we could follow the fellow who took it from her.'

Holmes considered, then asked, 'Are you actually volunteering to dress as a tramp and stand around near the flower seller for an hour or two, Watson?'

I was hurt by his implication that I might not be willing to perform any service helpful to our cause and said, warmly, 'Certainly, if it will help.'

My friend said, 'Then I thank you, my dear fellow, for your plan can do no harm and might possibly do some good.'

I had half hoped that he would turn down my offer but I could hardly wriggle out of it. Holmes laid the plan of action. 'Mr Forrage, you will take an envelope to the blind woman at about noon, telling her your name, which I am sure is all you will need to do. The envelope can be stuffed with pieces of paper to feel like banknotes, and securely sealed. As you turn to leave, Watson will start to lounge about in his disguise, as near to the flower seller as possible. Well, you both have your roles to enact and I am sure that Mr Forrage can arrange for your disguise in his theatrical department.'

As Holmes rose to leave us I dared to enquire, 'What will you be doing yourself?'

My friend assumed his most casual air and said, 'I, Watson, shall spend a diverting hour or two in the conjuring department. I will see you back at Baker Street for dinner and we will compare our experiences.'

Forrage was about to take me to his disguise section when a rather pronounced ticking noise, like a cheap alarm clock but louder, could plainly be heard. Forrage muttered and crossed to a rather strange-looking device which was standing upon a filing cabinet. The machine was emitting a ribbon of paper as it ticked. After a few seconds Forrage tore the ribbon from the machine and studied it. He looked back at us dolefully, and said, 'This is my latest toy, Holmes; it is rather like a telegraphy set-up. It conveys messages directly to me from certain centres. This one is from the Stock Exchange from whence I have received the tidings that the shares in A. W. Forrage Ltd have dropped in value, just at the time of year when one would expect them to go up. It has all leaked out, obviously. I could be ruined if this business does not become resolved. There is a board meeting tonight, and I have to tell my leading stockholders the bad news without being able to give them any sort of reason or excuse!'

I had never seen such a machine before, but had other things on my mind. Holmes made his way in the opposite direction to get the lift down to the first floor and the conjuring department as Forrage bundled me towards his theatrical area.

A young woman in an overall soon

managed to give me a suitably trampish complexion and headgear, but there was no tramp costume amongst the stock. However, Forrage managed to borrow some breeches and jacket from one of the gardeners on the roof. These doubtless once-natty garments gave me a definite air of being down on my luck.

I suppose 'A.W.' and I were an oddly assorted couple as we emerged from Forrage's and espied the flower seller from afar. Forrage said, 'I suggest, Watson, that you go first, just cross the road and hang about near the old woman. I'll follow and give her the envelope. Then, well, then it is up to you.'

I dodged the brewers' drays, taxi cabs and hansoms, not to mention one of the old horse buses and a motor car or two, in order to reach my goal. Then I looked back and noted with wonder how Forrage managed to cross the road entirely without difficulty. The sight of the famous A. W. Forrage was enough to make cabbies pull up their horses and motorists to drop their speed to almost nothing. I had heard the expression 'stopping the traffic' before but now I had witnessed a real demonstration!

Over what next occurred, dear reader, I will draw a veil, because you will hear of it in its right and proper place.

3

An Exchange of Experiences

'My dear Watson, what on earth has detained you?' My friend studied his watch and made clicking noises with his tongue as he rang for Mrs Hudson to bring the dinner. But I raised an admonishing hand and said, 'Holmes, surely you can see that I am not yet suitably attired for the dinner table. I must wash and change into more suitable clothing.'

I retired to remove my disguise and change into clean but comfortable apparel. As I took my place at the table, Holmes smiled benevolently at me and said, 'A great improvement, Watson, if a little below your normal sartorial standard. Why did you not change out of your tramp's clothing and back into your Saville Row grey, with the gloves and shoes from St James's before you returned?'

I stabbed a baked potato with my fork, angrily. There was nothing wrong with that roasted tuber, just with the sarcasm that my friend was playing out to me. I understood that he had a good idea as to the answers to his foolish questions, yet he insisted upon a full narration concerning all that had happened to me since he last saw me. I took a deep breath and despite the fact that I was still dining, I made a start, being direct and truthful despite the irony to which he had subjected me. 'Well, Holmes, once I had made a death-defying transference of myself to the opposite side of High Holborn to that occupied by Forrage's, I stationed myself near to the blind florist and watched 'A.W.' cross in his turn. He walked straight up to her, tipped his derby and handed her the padded-out envelope, tipped his hat again and retreated. Now she showed no surprise so obviously she was expecting him and the article in question. She placed it into a small box beneath her tiny stall and continued to implore passers-by to purchase her blooms, or 'pretty flahs' as she called them. Her trade was quite brisk, for she is good at her job. She speaks with a cajoling style that is hard to refuse in light of the darkened spectacles which she wears.

'I waited nearly an hour before anything of moment occurred. Then she quite deliberately and unexpectedly handed the envelope, or that which I took to be it, to a seedy-looking fellow dressed like a bookmaker. I made to shadow him, when to my amazement she handed another, exactly similar-looking padded envelope to a second shady-looking character!'

At this point I had eaten my fill and waved away an excellent fruit tart to smoke a pipe by the fireside. Holmes annoyed me by insisting on eating his fill at his own speed, so that I had to raise my voice a little to reach his ear across the room. I persevered. 'So you see I had no idea which of the two to follow, but just as I had decided to shadow the first man, a third presented himself, taking a flower, tendering a coin, and walking away with a *third* padded envelope. I tell you, Holmes, from the distance at which I stood, which by now was as close as I dared, it was impossible to tell which of these three envelopes was the one that Forrage had left her.'

Holmes had ceased at last, thankfully, to treat me like a child and, eyes wide with interest, joined me by the fire. I did not speak again until he had charged his pipe. Then once I knew that I had his full attention I continued. 'Then a woman, very smartly dressed, presented herself, purchased a bunch of flowers and got a padded envelope along with her change. I made a quick decision and started after her as discreetly as I was able. She crossed the road, and I thought at first she might enter Forrage's, but fortunately she did not. (I say fortunately, for I imagined I would have been ejected by a major domo had I attempted to enter the store in my tramp's attire.) Instead she passed the windows and made off towards New Oxford Street, stopping now and then to gaze into the odd shop window. She entered Smith's, the umbrella maker, and I waited around on the pavement. I pretended to be begging and someone actually dropped a penny into my outheld hat, saying, 'Do not spend it all at once, and do not use it to buy drink!' Then the woman, smart, youngish and dark, emerged with a brand new umbrella in a silver grey to match her coat.

'I again took to following her but then the worst possible thing happened. She suddenly stopped, turned, glared at me and said, 'Stop following me, you disgusting creature!' Did I say that it was the worst thing that happened? Well, it was just the start of a long run of bad luck. It so happened that a burly police constable was standing in a shop doorway and heard what she said to me. He stepped forward, his right hand descending upon my left shoulder. He saluted her and said, 'Don't worry, ma'am, I'll take care of his nibs here.' She smiled sweetly at him and went on her way.'

I paused, aware that my voice had begun to shake, as had my right hand which held my pipe. Holmes, to give him his due, instantly comforted me with a glass charged from the spirit flask and gasogene bottle. He said, 'My dear fellow, you really have suffered in my cause and I apologise for being the unwitting cause of these trials. Please compose yourself and then continue with your fascinating narrative.'

Kind words from Sherlock Holmes, and sincere ones at that, were rare and had the effect of soothing my frayed nerves. I continued my sad story. 'Well, I thought perhaps that the constable would utter some words of warning and that I would explain who I was, without of course bringing your name and present activities into it, and that I would be allowed to go on my way.'

'That was not the case?'

'No, instead he frogmarched me to the central West End police station, not listening to my excuses. He stood me in front of a sort of counter behind which sat a sergeant upon a high stool. That worthy listened to the constable's account of his reason for my arrest. Then he addressed me, saying, 'What have you got to say for yourself, cully?' I pulled myself up to my full height and said, 'I am an ex-army man, and a doctor of medicine, but just at the moment I am in disguise.' He grunted. 'Humph, very well-disguised if I may say so! Now listen to me, because you are an old soldier down on your luck I am going to let you go, as no actual charge has been made. But if we catch you begging or annoying anyone again it's chokey for you, my lad.' I tell you, Holmes, it was one of the most galling moments of my life as I walked out of the police station, realising that further argument would have led to my actual incarceration. I tell you, I say that even in this enlightened year of 1903, there is no justice for those who cannot present a respectable appearance.'

Holmes nodded. 'We are grateful for authorities such as the police force; it is only when one is misjudged by them that one realises how the poor and destitute live, without security or justice. But pray continue.'

'I walked in the direction of Forrage's, realising for the first time that I would only be able to enter that establishment with the utmost difficulty. I must trudge those heavy two miles, for I could hardly hail a cab or even ride an omnibus, having, as I thought, not the wherewithal to pay. Then fortunately my fingers stumbled upon the penny which I had been given when mistaken for a begger. So I climbed upon a 'bus and rode to Forrage's, being forced to sit on the open top with 'the other layabouts' as the conductor so charmingly put it. But alas, my troubles had only just begun. By the time I reached and alighted at the store it had closed; I had no way of obtaining admission or reclaiming my clothes. Moreover, I had spent my only penny and could only make the long trudge back here to Baker Street.'

There was a pause, then Holmes enquired, 'What did Mrs Hudson say when you presented yourself at the door? After all, you obviously had no keys save those still inside Forrage's.'

I told him that which I really wished to forget. 'She refused to recognise me or let me in for a full two minutes. Then I managed to shift some of the cosmetic dirt upon my face.'

Holmes handed me another drink and said, 'My dear fellow, what a truly horrific experience. I mean, things just seemed to get worse as time passed . . . '

Suddenly he ceased to speak and a strange gasping and wheezing emanated from his throat. I thought at first he had suddenly become asthmatic; instead the sound was the prelude to the rarest sounds of all, the hearty laughter of Sherlock Holmes! When he was again able to speak he said, 'Oh, my dear Watson, I do apologise, but I just cannot control myself, with the mental picture of you begging in the street, and being arrested and . . . oh dear . . . '

He had started to laugh again, but this time he did not laugh alone, for I had quite regained my sense of humour. It was a full quarter of an hour of the clock before we were both in full control of ourselves. Then, as we recovered, I asked, 'But what of your own adventures, Holmes, how did you spend your afternoon?'

He shook his head. 'Nowhere near as

entertainingly as your own experiences, Watson, but there were developments, I assure you. Yes, there were developments.'

He sat back in his chair and played out his story, like a playwright trying to intrigue an actor-manager.

'I left Forrage to spend an interesting couple of hours in the conjuring department. You know, Watson, I have spent most of my adult life in solving mysteries, yet when faced with a first-class conjurer, I am as putty in his hands. I honestly believe that if one of these worthies turned to crime, with his misdirection and deft sleight of hand he would be as formidable an adversary as I have faced. A sort of magical Moriarty, a Maskelyne of wrongdoers. At first I stood well back and enjoyed the experience of seeing the children laughing and gasping in turns as the demonstrator caught silver coins from out of the thin air and made a shower of comfits appear in a singularly innocent-looking glass vase. I was surprised to learn that quite such impressive 'miracles' were for sale. But when I learned of the prices charged I realised that the idly curious would be scarcely likely to buy them. Indeed, most of the customers, and trade was brisk, were distinctly theatrical-looking, some of them even sporting fierce waxed moustaches and sharply pointed goatees. Now and then there would be a jolly uncle type who obviously was not a theatrical but wished to impress his nephews with a performance on Boxing Day. These mostly purchased trick boxes and tubes of which even I had some inkling as to their mechanics.

'There was a lull in the activity at around five, and I managed to engage the demonstrator in conversation. His name was Collins and he told me that the department had a brand new manager, a Mr Will Goldston, lately arrived from Liverpool in which great city he had been operating his own magical emporium, numbering among his customers the Great Houdini, Horace Goldin and a Mr Carl Hertz, all of whom I was assured are professional illusionists at the very peak of their calling. Mr Collins was a dapper man with a well-trained moustache and an engagingly precise manner. He was good enough to introduce me to the celebrated Mr Goldston who emerged from behind a glass door, which evidently housed a cupboard of a department manager's office. He was surprisingly young for his high position, being I would judge no more than about five and twenty though deceptively bald. He proved to be a shrewd man who had drawn his own conclusions from the rumoured troubles of which he had heard. He recognised me, unfortunately, from Paget's illustrations to your sensationalised accounts of my exploits but I feel that I can trust him to keep his own counsel regarding our involvement.'

Holmes appeared to have spent a far more congenial afternoon and evening than had I. He continued. 'No doubt you are thinking that I simply spent my time in unfettered enjoyment of the entertainment provided and in such congenial company whilst you suffered your indignities?'

I nodded. 'Well, Holmes, you have rather read my mind.'

'Ah, Watson, I weep for you, as the walrus said, I deeply sympathise. But I have not finished the account of my adventures yet. You see, something occurred which proved my attention to the threatened department was warranted. Not long before the closing bell a rather singular event was to occur. A man of rather theatrical appearance entered upon the scene and demanded of Mr Collins a demonstration of that which he called 'The clay pipes mystery'. Collins nodded and picked up two clay pipes from behind the counters and blew through each in turn indicating that both were empty of bowl and free of obstruction. He then placed the two bowls together and produced clouds of smoke, but rather spoiled the effect of it all by coughing, spluttering and ultimately collapsing to the ground. Goldston soon had him up and seated upon a chair and caused a glass of water to be brought.

'As Collins slowly recovered, Goldston turned to me and said, 'Such an experienced demonstrator, but anyone can make a mistake. You see, Mr Holmes, there are two boxes of clay pipes behind the counter. Box A contains pipes, the bowls of which have been treated with ammonia. In box B are pipes with bowls that have been similarly treated with hydrochloric acid. As a student of chemistry you will understand that when the bowls are placed together clouds of smoke will result, which, if not inhaled can be taken into the mouth and blown forth by the demonstrator. However, in so doing he must be careful not to suck in upon the pipe that has been treated with the acid. You have seen what can happen if a mistake is made.'

'Collins had recovered enough to splutter, 'I made no mistake: the wrong pipe was in the ammonia box!'

'Goldston examined the boxes of pipes and discovered that all of the ammonia treated pipes were in box B and vice versa. I suggested, 'An easy mistake surely, for if the back of the counter were to be tidied by an underling the pipes might get into the wrong boxes?'

'Both conjurers shook their heads.

Goldston explained, 'As an added precaution the pipes are individually marked 'H' for the acid and 'A' for ammonia. Step round here, Holmes, and see for yourself.'

'I did as he bade me and applied the nose test, finding that his words were true. The pipes were not only in their wrong boxes but were falsely marked, as applying each to my nose proved. Need I say that I enquired as to from whence the prepared pipes were obtained and was told that they came from one of a number of outworkers, whose supplies had always proved satisfactory in the past. I obtained his address and I may well interview him, yet I was, and am, more interested in those intermediate stages which the stock passes through betwixt maker and retail counter. In the case of the conjuring department the path was a winding one. From past experience and present need Goldston has a file of people who specialise in the manufacture of certain conjuring accessories and apparatus. For example, he has a carpenter with a long experience of making various trick boxes.

Another worker makes trick metal frames and tripod tables. He has a specialist in the adulteration of playing cards and of course the man who supplies the chemical mysteries.'

I interrupted. 'So these people sell the goods to Forrage's?'

Holmes smiled enigmatically. 'It is not quite so simple, Watson; the makers sell the goods in the first place to a sort of magical wholesale firm in Liverpool, Devo Enterprises.'

'Then Devo Enterprises sell the goods to Forrage's?'

'Be patient, Watson. Devo sells the goods to a London wholesaler of magical goods, Leah Laurie Ltd. In turn they are purchased by Blandford Street Magic who add such niceties as printed instructions before selling them to Forrage's. The printing is supplied by Aladdin Impress Ltd and all of the firms and companies that I have mentioned have something in common.'

'That they deal in conjuring goods?'

'More. That Will Goldston is a director of each save Leah Laurie Ltd, which is owned by Mrs Goldston, whose professional name is Leah Laurie!'

'Is all this legal, Holmes?'

'Perfectly, Watson.'

'Does Forrage know of it?'

'I doubt it.'

'Shall you tell him?'

'Oh, I think not, Watson, I can use his co-operation and his diplomacy concerning my enquiries.'

I grunted. 'Smacks of blackmail.'

'Smacks more of mutual assistance, Watson.'

I considered. 'Well, you have certainly established that Goldston is a bit sharp to say the least. Does he have no ideas concerning the threats and this one that was actually carried out in his own department?'

'Let me just say that he has been extremely helpful and has given me much food for thought.'

'I suppose you will keep a sharp eye on developments in the conjuring department?'

'Not especially. Goldston will do that, and if the pattern is followed, another department will receive the attention of our enemy next.'

★   ★   ★

On the following day we consulted A. W. Forrage again and told him something of our adventures. He knew already of the events in the conjuring department of course, but we could tell that Goldston had given him a rather mild version of them. The conjuring manager was a diplomat, loyal to his promises, but also anxious concerning a managerial position which enabled him to earn a good wage and commission on goods that he sold, having already gained a profit of some kind on them at several other stages of their existence.

Forrage told us that no fresh threats had been received by himself but was pessimistic concerning the future. 'Mr Holmes, over the past couple of days you have observed several dramatic events take place, events of which you had been warned as I had. You have expounded shrewdly upon these events, yet you seem helpless to prevent such things happening. What exactly is your role if you cannot stop these dreadful things?'

I felt his remarks to be unfair to my colleague and said, 'Oh, come, sir, despite the annoying nature of these events, no serious damage has been done to person or property.'

He retorted, 'Quite so, Dr Watson, but for how long can I keep such happenings out of the newspapers, and who is to say that they will not take a more serious turn? The fellow, whoever he is, may be lulled into a feeling of security which will embolden him; especially if he learns that he has fooled even the great Sherlock Holmes.'

My friend was never a man to be browbeaten and he spoke warmly but politely to the famous store magnate. 'My dear Forrage, to round on me thus is your privilege, but I have learned during some twenty years of crime detection that one gets the best from a hireling by encouragement rather than from words of chastisement. I expect to tie up this matter within a matter of days. However, you are free to dispense with my services if you wish. In arguing with me you are wasting my time, and also your own. I have certain investigations which I intend to make; I will inform you concerning these tomorrow.'

Sherlock Holmes took a polite but icy farewell of Forrage, and we left the splendid office for . . . I knew not where.

As we made our way to the main front entrance to the building, Holmes gave me some idea of his immediate plans. 'We will follow up on your escapade of yesterday, Watson. Your disguise and clandestine activities did no good so let us see what will happen if we tackle the flower woman quite openly.'

We crossed High Holborn and made for the flower stall but found an elderly man tending it. He was a sharp-looking customer dressed in a jacket that was checked like a draughts board. His billycock was worn at an angle and I considered that despite his age he could have been an unwelcome man to bump into on a dark night. Once he realised that we were not customers, his expression of cherubic innocence changed to one of irritation. He said, 'I don't know where the old girl has gone. I heard she was ill and I at once meant to offer to open her stall lest she lose her pitch. But there was nobody at her place, so I'm just keeping the stall warm for her.'

I ventured, 'Perhaps she has been taken to hospital?'

He answered, 'Naah, I'd have heard!'

Holmes handed the man a half sovereign and his whole attitude changed.

'Well now, gents, let me see . . . she could be staying with her sister at the buildings in Clerkenwell Road. Other than that I can't think where she could be. But I'll give you the address and if you manage to get hold of her you can tell her that Joe is looking after her gaff. Mind you, she'll need to get back soon as I'm running out of flowers.'

Holmes had obtained from Joe not only the flower lady's sister's address, but also that at which he knew her normally to reside. This was in a mean street off Hatton Garden, in sharp contrast with the business thoroughfare which housed the diamond merchants of the largest city in the world. It was an attic apartment that we made for, to find a rat-infested staircase and no answer to our knock upon the dilapidated front door. Sherlock Holmes lifted the letterbox flap with his cane and sank to his knees to peer through it. He appeared surprised at what he saw.

'A mean street and a less than modest attic apartment from the outside. Yet within it is surprisingly well furnished; at least as far as the entrance area is concerned.'

In my turn I glanced through the flap and started at the sight of surprisingly well made and expensive-looking hall-stand and chairs. A rug upon the floor appeared to be also of good quality. However, there is often a simple enough explanation for such things and I remarked, 'Perhaps the flower business is more profitable than might be supposed. If so, the lady certainly does not spend her money on a high rental and might well be able to indulge a desire for good furnishings.'

Holmes grunted. 'You may be right, Watson, that may explain it, and we had better visit her sister who may enlighten us more.'

4

The Basement of Wonder

Little was gained from our visit to the apartment in the Clerkenwell Road where we did indeed find the flower lady's sister. She was a jolly woman, who told us, 'Nothing mysterious. Nelly has gone for a few days' holiday to Yarmouth where we have a cousin. Tell old Joe that I'll be round in the morning to see about the stall. I'm not surprised that he sent someone else, he and I don't get on too well, but I'm surprised that he managed to get a couple of swells like you to run his errands!'

Holmes did some quick thinking and said, 'We are from the Holborn Town Hall, we have been asked to inspect your sister's permit to sell flowers opposite Forrage's.'

She took a frame down from the wall which housed such a document. 'There it is. Nelly keeps it here because her place is none too safe. I've asked her to move in here with Tom and me, but she is that independent she is. But at least I've got her to accept a few bits and pieces from this flat that I was going to sling out. Suppose you are going to ask me how I managed to furnish this place so nice? Well, Tom has a good job and when mum died she left me some money, not a fortune but enough to indulge me fancies. She left nothing to Nelly because she was always ashamed of her selling things in the street; you know how snobbish old women can be. Well, I look after Nelly because I feel that she ought to have got some of the money. Anyway aside from that, she is my sister.'

As we made our way back to High Holborn I suggested that the woman had seemed quite respectable and sensible. Holmes agreed; he had not brought up the matter of Forrage and the envelope, saying, 'There seemed little point and we would have needed to put our cards upon the table to ask her that. This I feel unwilling to do at this exact moment. But we need to be able to give Forrage some scrap of encouragement soon, Watson.'

We had no lead to follow and as if by habit it seemed to me we turned into the front entrance of Forrage's. The store was packed with shoppers and browsers, and even those who were simply mildly curious. We decided to take a lift to the second floor and explore some of those departments that we had neglected so far. The office supplies department seemed less crowded than most of the others, but then filing cabinets and stationery were never high on the average Christmas list. We admired the rows of shining, brand-new typewriting machines and a strange-looking device which we were assured was a 'Dictagram'. One spoke into a tube-shaped object, light enough to be held in the hand, which was attached to a machine which looked like a rather large gramophone, fitted with the old-fashioned cylinder. The salesman explained, 'You speak into the tube and your voice is recorded upon the cylinder. In a year or two I imagine it will use the new flat discs that the latest gramophones utilise. Meanwhile, the cylinder is very practical and can be used over and over again to play back your messages. Would you care to try it?'

I spoke a few words which I heard repeated as if from afar and through a muffin, but had to admit that for dictation purposes it would be quite practical. Holmes seemed uninterested, glancing around the rest of the wares whilst I was so engaged.

As we sauntered away, through the luggage department, Holmes asked me if I had seen or heard anything of significance in Office Supplies. I told him that I could not honestly say that I had, but that I had found the new dictation machine of interest. He shrugged and said, 'When it is half the size and twice as accurate I will purchase one, for I can see its value. But there were other things in that department which interested me, for example . . .'

But he was interrupted. A. W. Forrage suddenly appeared and hailed us. 'Holmes, I'm glad to run into you . . . another threat has arrived, typed on a folded paper just as before.'

He thrust a now familiar-looking folded sheet into my friend's hand and stood by in a very agitated manner. Holmes indicated the Café Continental entrance and suggested that we retreat therein to examine the missive. Forrage agreed and ordered coffee for us, but not until it had been delivered to our fairly secluded alcove did he again bring back the subject. 'Well, Holmes, what do you make of it?'

My friend studied it and passed it to me, saying to Forrage, 'It's meaning is clear but not of course the degree of its threat.'

I read the message aloud quietly,

WITH SAWDUST A CIRCLE WITHOUT END? IT MAY END IN TEARS.

Forrage asked, 'D'ye reckon he refers to the tool department? You know, saws and sawdust and all that?'

Holmes shook his head. 'I believe it refers to a sawdust ring, the circus in your basement.'

We finished our coffee swiftly and made our way, the three of us, to the basement.

It had been quite a few years since I had seen a circus and the one in Forrage's store was very small in comparison to those that I remembered from my youth. But I must say that from the point of view of quality and smartness it compared favourably. The area which Forrage told me was often deployed as a 'bargain basement' outside of the Christmas season had been quite transformed. There was a circle of tiered seating for about three hundred people, surrounding a sawdust ring of about eighteen feet across. Holmes informed me that this was only about three-quarters of the size of a full circus ring. Sometimes I wondered how he managed to absorb and remember such trivialities. There was a smart ring entrance, like a miniature theatre with red plush curtains atop of which sat four musicians in military uniforms. They played brass instruments with verve if not expertise.

I will not tire the reader with a

description of the performance as a whole: enough to mention a few high-lights just to give some idea of the character of the event itself. First, however, let me say that like everything else at Forrage's it was rattling good value for the few pence charged for admission. It was brief of duration, being little more than an hour in length, but any child who had never seen a circus would have enjoyed an excellent taste of what such an entertainment could offer with its trained horses, acrobats and clowns, and perhaps most surprising of all a real live elephant which walked upon a huge ball and lathered and shaved one of the clowns. Finally the elephant trainer explained to the audience that the huge pachyderm would walk over the recumbent form of the trainer's wife 'Maritza', and he called for complete and utter silence during the feat, saying, 'I do not wish anything to happen to Maritza, because it took me a long time to find her!'

This charming little speech brought a round of applause and this was followed by the silence appealed for as the ponderous great animal stepped daintily with each great foot over the recumbent Maritza. There was a gasp of relief when it was all over and the first of the several daily performances was complete. As the audience trooped out, Holmes, Forrage and I conferred.

'I think we need to pay serious attention to that final feat for a number of reasons,' said Holmes.

I said, 'You mean because it is the most dangerous moment in the performance?'

'Yes, but also because the threat mentions 'MAY END IN TEARS'. The feat is not only dangerous but is at the very end of the circus. Forrage, I would like to talk to the elephant trainer.'

He was hesitant. 'You may do so, but I must ask that you be diplomatic. Do not either cause him to become anxious, or yet inform him of the purpose of your enquiries.'

Holmes nodded and replied, 'I have carried out, sir, investigations which involved royal houses and upon the outcome of these investigations, in some instances, the fate of nations and many thousands of lives depended.'

Holmes was furious, I could tell, from his icy calm manner, and did not wait for a reply as he strode towards the curtained entrance with Forrage and me in his wake.

As we passed through that red plush curtain we were 'back-stage' at the circus in fact, but not in feeling. I had once been behind the scenes at a circus in a big tent on Clapham Common as a child. The atmosphere had been something that I had never forgotten with the smell of fresh grass mixed with that of the sawdust and alfresco stables. Here one could not forget that one was in the basement of a huge department store, with the odours generated by the beasts being dulled with perfumed disinfectant. But as for the cast of clowns and artistes, they were a different matter and spoke to each other in that international language of the sawdust ring; thus Hungarians under-stood Swedes and English acrobats could call to French musicians that their music was wrong. Holmes spoke to the Hungar-ian elephant trainer, assuming the role of an inspector from the league to protect captive animals. He explained, 'Mr Kover, I have brought my veterinary surgeon, Mr West, to examine your elephant.'

I started, for aside from the fact that the elephant was of the Asiatic variety, I had little experience to call upon. I asked him to cause the animal to open its mouth and pretended to look at its teeth. Fortunately I remembered from my days in India that elephants during their time upon this earth are blessed with a number of sets of molars; not just two sets as with homo sapiens. I enquired, 'Are these her third or fourth set of teeth?'

Kover replied, 'Her fourth, for she is fifty years of age.'

I grunted, walked around the beast nodding wisely, and then turned to Holmes saying, 'The animal appears to be in good condition, Mr Summers.'

Holmes did not start at the name with which I had retaliated and said, 'I think we can give this three-ton lady a good report, Kover, and I hope for the sake of your good lady that the animal has a steady temperament.'

Then he questioned the trainer regarding the degree of danger involved with the feat that we had just witnessed. 'Your wife is, I trust, not in real peril when the animal walks over her?'

Kover answered in a very direct manner. 'Oh no, sir, I would not permit that. There is a certain risk, but then we are circus people. The appeal for silence is just for show, a sweet bag or a child crying would not cause Mitzie to step upon Maritza. It would take a very great disturbance to do that.'

I asked, 'Perhaps an explosion or something of the kind?'

He replied, 'That at the least, Mr West.'

We took our leave of Kover and his wife and, of course, his elephant Mitzie and mingled with some of the other artistes and grooms, with Holmes and I keeping up our characters as vet and inspector. My friend, I soon realised, was trying to discover if any of the circus people had noticed anyone of unusual character hanging around the enterprise. He particularly asked such questions of the clown whom we had observed to spend a deal of time in the audience. He asked, 'My dear Mr Bimbo, during your excursions among the spectators, have you seen anyone of a kind that you would not expect to encounter in a circus audience?'

The clown nodded. 'Come to think of it there has been a chap, rough-looking, at several performances. He did not seem terribly interested in what he saw: never laughed when I handed him my imitation red hot poker to hold, and when the acrobats were on he seemed to be looking everywhere except at the ring.'

'He has caused no trouble, no disturbance?'

'Oh no, sir, he just sits quiet, on the top tier opposite the ring entrance.'

We emerged back into the store itself and Holmes turned to me to say, 'Watson, we will occupy seats in that top tier ourselves at the very next performance. We might yet avert a tragedy, for I feel that this latest threat is intended to warn of more than mere inconvenience.'

We dallied a while in the pet and

livestock department during the time we had free before the second circus performance. I suppose you could have called what we experienced a glorified pet shop. But its scale was considerable with the tiger cub as the central point of interest. However, there were aviaries and aquaria with all the usual birds and fish, and white mice beloved of the schoolboy. Parrots and macaws were tethered upon stands and dozens of rabbits and guinea pigs roamed free in a large pen. Of course, a big store has a jungle drum system of communication and although we had roamed quietly around the emporium a number of times before we had never until that actual day assumed characters that might be remembered. 'Summers and West' were now known to be inspectors of livestock, and the manager of the pet department not only knew us but treated us with a certain amount of apprehension.

'Everything all right, gents? You will find everything here is done for the comfort of our little guests. They may not be long with us, but I'll wager these are the best days of their lives. I hate to sell an animal that I have got to know, and I can always tell what sort of a home they are going to. Why, the posh kid who is getting the tiger cub for Christmas will soon get sick of it, and his father will blanche at having to buy it twelve pounds of meat a day when it grows up! As for the poor fish, they will last about a week at most in those wretched little bowls that I am forced to sell. I can tell you this because I know you are not with the firm. But between ourselves, I don't think old man Forrage gives a tinker's cuss about the creatures, aside from the profit they bring. I went to him once, 'Mr Forrage', I said, 'someone should be in the store on Sundays to feed and clean out the animals.' But he just turned to me and said, 'Just do your job.' He doesn't care I tell you . . . '

I picked up a rabbit and pretended to examine it, pronouncing it to be in splendid condition, and hoping that it was. Then I returned it to the pen and said, 'Well done, sir, I can see that you are a humane man and an animal lover.'

We repaired to the circus again and sat just where we had determined to. Between scanning the spectators for the rough type that the clown had described, we discussed our dalliance among the pets. I asked, 'Did you notice how he shook with suppressed rage when he spoke of Forrage?'

Holmes replied, 'It could hardly go unobserved. Moreover, it does not sound as if Forrage is very fond of the poor man either. His name is Greenford by the way.'

'Oh, did he tell you, I did not hear . . . '

'No, I observed the badge pinned onto his dustcoat; you were convincing as a veterinary person, but you will never make a detective.'

Well, Holmes was always very variable in his praise or otherwise of my efforts to aid his deductions. Only a day or two earlier he had said to me, 'We will make a detective of you yet', but I was used to his stick-and-carrot use of praise and ridicule. I concentrated upon my task as an observer.

Dear reader, I will not bore you with a description of the scale of our scanning and the duration of it. Enough to say that we had wasted our time in attending that particular performance. However, by repeating the operation at the final performance of the day we gained some result. The man who had taken our attention had slipped in just as the lights in the audience were lowered and those illuminating the sawdusted circle were raised. But before the gloom had enveloped us we had gained time to observe the roughly-dressed individual, sporting a peaked cap and green pea-jacket. The lighting of the circus varied, being raised in the auditorium whenever the clown Bimbo made an excursion among the crowd. During one of these interludes he spotted us and rolled his eyes in the direction of the rough-looking man, as if to say, 'That's him!' Then he doffed his fool's cap and started to place it upon the heads of children and even adults in turn. I rather fancy I cut a dash in it, but it made Sherlock Holmes look ridiculous. Then as he tried to remove the rough man's cap to replace it with the cone of white felt, the fellow waved him aside in a curt manner, accidentally jostling the person who sat between us. The jostled one decided to move his seat and left the row altogether leaving a space where he had been seated.

As it happens this proved providential.

When the final act, that of the elephant, was arrived at, I noted that the fellow seated near me changed his hunched attitude to one of alertness and thrust his hands deep into the pockets of his pea-jacket. Holmes whispered to me to sidle up to the rough man and he, himself, walked along the row to the far side of him. He caused other spectators to move along the bench and he sat so that our quarry was wedged between us.

'Mitzie, hup!'

The elephant trainer called once again for silence and the lumbering animal started to raise a tree trunk of a leg. Then suddenly I detected a rapid movement from the man sandwiched between us, and immediately Holmes was wrestling with his right arm. He hissed, 'Watson, grab his left arm!'

I did as he bade me, but the fellow

wriggled free of us, to drop through the gap near the seating footboard, seven or eight feet to the ground below. I was all for pursuit but Holmes whispered, 'Not the right time for a disturbance, Watson!'

The great detective sat as if frozen, until the elephant had finished her traversal of the prone figure of the elephant trainer's wife. Then, as she arose, smiling, arms held high and the applause broke out, he said, 'Thank heaven there was a minimum of commotion. You see, Watson, the fellow had a pistol, but I managed to wrest it from him.'

He showed me the small, neat weapon which he now held. I gasped. 'Great Scott! Did he mean to shoot the lady or the elephant?'

Despite the gravity of the situation, Holmes chuckled. 'Neither, Watson. If you examine the pistol you will find that it is made entirely in order to fire blank cartridges, with which it is loaded. No, he meant to make a maximum of disturbance, enough to startle the elephant into dropping a foot upon the intrepid Maritza.'

It soon became clear that the 'assassin' had planned to drop to the ground, as he indeed had, to escape under cover of the tumult that he would have caused. As it was he had escaped without chase. I said, 'A pity we did not manage to hold him.'

Holmes said, 'The struggle was not worth the risk, and in any case he was not our man; simply a pawn in the game, I'll wager.'

As the national anthem was played and we all stood to attention, I espied at least one figure moving within the circus. It was A. W. Forrage himself, seeking us, and as the final notes of 'God Save the Queen' emerged from trumpet and trombone he espied us and started to climb up the steps to the top tier.

'There was a rough fellow who streaked out of the circus like a bat out of hell! Has the threatened tragedy occurred?'

He stood at the end of the row of plank seating, obviously very concerned with a touch of anger in that concern. But Holmes spoke softly with his inevitable incisive thrust. 'On the contrary, my dear

Forrage, a tragedy has been averted, thanks to the most part for the prompt actions performed by your hired investigators; in short our good selves.'

His irony was not lost on Forrage who became calm of manner as Holmes and I, taking turn and turn about, managed to give him an accurate account of the happenings of the past quarter of an hour. He breathed hard, for apology did not come easily to the store magnate, but apologise he did. 'I am sorry. I am so used to events transpiring where there is no seeming redress that I made a wrong assumption. You have done well, Holmes, to prevent what could well have been a tragic event.'

Holmes nodded curtly and said, 'Your apology is duly noted, and let us hope that we have at last turned the corner in our pursuit of your tormentor, and that we may soon be able to tell you that we have discovered his, or her, identity.'

Forrage started, 'You do not mean to suggest that there is a possibility, however remote, that this evil being could be a woman?'

Holmes chuckled. 'My dear sir, the female of the species can be deadlier than the male. We have seen only one of your ill-wisher's minions. Whilst I have no particular reason to suspect that it is a woman, I cannot discount the possibility.'

When we had parted with Forrage, I turned to Holmes and asked, 'Holmes, do you have any reason to suspect that our adversary is female?'

He chuckled. 'None whatever, but my dear Watson one has to give the client a run for his money, so to speak. He will be back in his office by now, wondering why his wife, his secretary or his mother-in-law should be tormenting him.'

I remarked accusingly and not for the first time, 'Holmes, you have a certain cruel streak of irony at times, which I might add is quite unworthy of you.'

My friend nodded with mock severity as he said, 'You are, of course, right, but we cannot all be paragons of human virtue like yourself, my dear Watson!'

5

The Early Riser

On the following morning I determined to rise early, aspiring even to be the first to the breakfast table. As I walked into the dining room to see our places both neatly laid and undisturbed, I felt that my determination had paid off, if the reader will forgive me for using the parlance of 'the sport of kings'. But alas the best laid plans of mice and men . . . what?

There was the sound of the front door opening, footfalls which gave me to believe that we had an early visitor, yes, early indeed. In my mind I deduced that he was a man of some eleven stone and a half, of middle years but energetic, rather like Sherlock Holmes himself. My deductions could not have been more accurate for the door to the apartment opened and the fellow entered unannounced: which was scarcely surprising as he turned out to be Sherlock Holmes himself.

'My dear Watson, I rose early and took the opportunity to use the newly installed telephone at the post office. Have you used it yet? It is quite an experience; rather like conversing with an Edison-Bell phonograph cylinder. But when you consider that I was speaking to someone at a distance of some four to five miles it is hardly surprising. The post master assures me that very soon one will be able to converse with someone who is at least ten miles away and within a decade every business and government department will be able to be reached by telephone. Eventually I have no doubt that the ordinary people will be able to install such an instrument in their homes. Alas, I shall not be here to see it, or rather hear it.'

This was the first time that I had heard my friend speak of himself as other than indestructible. I was concerned. I said, 'Why, Holmes, you are scarcely middle-aged. Come, there are quite a few years left in you, always assuming that you do not resume some of your earlier bad habits!'

He chuckled, but not, I would learn, at my reference to his one-time regular use of cocaine. He said, 'You are right, Watson, but you see I was referring to my residence in this apartment. I meant that I would not be here long enough to see a telephone installed: I did not hint at my early demise.'

I was relieved, but puzzled. 'You have never given me the slightest hint that you intended moving house.'

'Have I not mentioned an intention to retire to the Sussex coast to keep bees and have time to meditate upon my own thoughts, Watson?'

He had indeed vaguely mentioned such intentions from time to time, but I had assumed that he had referred to some kind of preparation for his old age. I said, 'Yes, but an active man such as yourself does not contemplate retirement when still short of fifty years! I had assumed that you were making prediction of events for the year 1920, or thereabouts.'

I realised that he was quite serious as

he replied, 'I am still I believe, as I speak, at the very height of my mental and physical powers. But five or seven years from now I might still believe this and be a victim of self-deception. I have made a reputation and have helped a great many people, some of them at their wit's end. They have trusted me and thankfully I have managed to justify their trust. I dare not risk in the future some poor wretch depending upon a Sherlock Holmes that is past his best without realising it. As I say, my reputation is important too. With all this in mind I may from this time take on few if any new cases. The affair at Forrage's may well be Sherlock Holmes's last escapade!'

Then his eyes twinkled as he added, 'So make the most of it for the enjoyment of your readers. If I do not solve the problem for Forrage you will, of course, have no story to tell and I will have retired not a moment too soon. If I do solve it, though, I fear it will be quite a few years before you can lay the episode before your avid public.'

But I was less concerned for my literary

career than I was for Holmes's future plans. We had been friends and colleagues for a very long time, at least twenty years, and I could not imagine my life without the excitement, admiration, wonder and occasional anger that Sherlock Holmes had brought to it. I suppose this is hardly entirely true, because I had that period when I had believed him dead to suggest the mediocrity which the future might hold. But I realised that I could not dwell upon morbid thoughts and must back up my friend to the last.

'Might one enquire who it was that you spoke to upon this telephonic marvel?'

'I don't think you have met an acquaintance of mine, Gregory Kline, who works for a finance company in the city? I wanted his opinion upon the situation at Forrage's. For example, who would gain from its descent to a lower position in the world of retail fame. He could think of nobody, but he gave me quite a lot of information regarding the way the store is organised and so on. I will not bore you with the trivial, Watson, but it appears that Forrage has some very shrewd fellow stockholders of whom he needs to be ever wary. I could have called upon Kline as I have on previous occasions, but I just wanted to try out this telephone and judge its usefulness for myself. Watson, I do believe that if I did not contemplate retirement, I would move heaven and earth to get one installed here at 221B.'

This of course was typical of Sherlock Holmes; he had ever been the first to try an innovation. He had sent wires as if they were postcards and I had noted of late that he had taken to writing with a patent contraption which held its own reservoir of ink. Yet I knew that he bemoaned the inevitable passing of the hansom cab. (There were plenty of them still upon the London streets, but it was becoming obvious that the motorised taxicab would eventually drive them off the roads.) However, his lament had practicality behind it. One can ride in a hansom and preserve one's anonymity: a taxicab attracts attention and is without curtains. The top half of the hansom provides a gloom which obscures one's identity.

But I digress, dear reader, and must take up my story from the point where we both sat down to breakfast. Holmes eager for his refreshment through an appetite created by an early excursion, whilst I was as ever ready for my favourite meal of the day. A forkful of bacon was about to be inserted into my eager mouth when I heard the doorbell. This was followed by the faithful steps of Mrs Hudson as she descended the stairs. Then her footfalls were accompanied upon her return by those of a youthful person. I asked, 'One of the irregulars?'

Holmes replied, 'I doubt it, most of them are grown and dispersed, and those that remain would not be able to resist a scamper up the steps, even under Mrs Hudson's stern gaze. This youth has the joyless step of a messenger.'

'A boy with a wire?'

'No, he has not those heavy official boots . . .'

The door opened and the good house-keeper announced, 'Boy from Forrage's, Mr Holmes, says he has a message. His boots are fairly clean.'

Holmes chuckled. 'Send him in then, Mrs Hudson, as he seems to have passed your inspection.'

A downtrodden-looking youth entered, holding an envelope. He wore thick spectacles through which he squinted at us in turn.

'One of you gents Sherlock 'Olmes? Only I was ordered to deliver this personal.'

My friend rose and took the envelope, saying, 'I am he, the very same. Pray be seated, young man, whilst I see if a reply is required. Watson, pray pour our friend a cup of coffee and for heaven's sake, do something about his spectacles!'

I lifted the wire-rimmed glasses from the boy's face and examined them. The boy was docile and allowed me to do this without making a scene. Indeed he said, 'My eyes is troubling me something terrible, it seems to be getting worse.'

As if to illustrate he picked up the milk

jug in mistake for his coffee cup. I studied the spectacles and soon realised that they might not have been cleaned since they had been fashioned. I held them over the vapour from the coffee pot and then cleaned the lenses with my table napkin. Within a few seconds they were crystal clear and I returned them to the boy. He replaced them on his nose and gasped, 'I can see . . . I can see!'

I chuckled and said, 'It well may continue thus if you clean them, at least once each day.'

He gasped, 'I didn't realise that you 'ad to clean 'em.'

He was, I realised, a particularly dense youngster. In my youth we might have described him as 'only about eightpence in the shilling'.

Holmes did not interest himself in the drama of the short-sighted youth and his occular improvement. He was busy scribbling an obviously terse note on the back of one of his visiting cards. He placed the pasteboard into a small envelope upon which he wrote the name 'A. W. Forrage, Esquire', handing it to the transformed youth who grinned as he peered at the name on the envelope.

'It's for the old man, eh? Cor, when he knows I can read again perhaps I will get promoticated!'

I stifled a chuckle, until his footsteps were heard upon the stairs with their renewed elasticity and the front door had banged shut. Holmes said, 'Upon my word, let us hope that his rediscovered reading talent does not lead him to *The Strand* magazine.'

I said, 'More like *Aly Sloper's Half Holiday*!'

Holmes admonished me. 'Really, Watson, you show your age. That particular juvenile journal is long extinct. But I'll wager he follows the exploits of 'Weary Willie and Tired Tim' in *Chips*!'

Sherlock Holmes never ceased to amaze me with the fingers that he kept upon the public pulse. But I suppose a knowledge of modern juvenilia was as important to him as his background in the classics. All is grist to the investigator's mill.

'Friend Forrage has received another

threat, Watson, and you will see that it is again typed upon a similar sheet of paper and neatly folded.'

My breakfast had, of course, been ruined, so I pushed aside my now cold platter of bacon, eggs and sausages. I spread the note which had been passed to me carefully upon the unspoiled portion of the table cloth and took also the lens which he passed to me. I could see that the type was pristine as before and the paper was of the same make. It read,

BEWARE THE IDES OF MARCH

It was even more terse than its forerunners, and less easy to understand as to meaning. I said, 'It is a Shakespearean quotation, of course, but how it can be applied to a department store in November is beyond me.'

'Do you know what an 'ide' is, Watson?'

'Something to do with the calendar?' I said, vaguely.

He shook his head. 'An 'ide' is the archaic name for a small fish. Scholars of

Shakespearean English have long disagreed as to whether it refers to a minnow or a stickleback.'

I remembered fishing with a net for such tiny fish as a lad, but had not realised that they were of several kinds, referring to each darting silvery prize as a 'tiddler'. I remarked, 'When I was a boy I kept them in jamjars; some of them had red around their fore fins.'

'Those were sticklebacks; the red only appears during the breeding season when they will fight all other small fish to the death. Despite their extremely small size they have razor sharp teeth. I have, as you saw, sent a message to Forrage to the effect that we will be with him at midday. That will give us a little time to try and earn our crust.'

So the reader will appreciate that the best laid plans of your humble scribe concerning early to rise were completely spoiled, certainly playing no part in making me healthy, wealthy or yet particularly wise. We donned our hats and greatcoats and bundled into the first cab that appeared which happened to be a motor taxi. I caught Holmes's eye as we sped toward Holborn. He said, 'You need not say anything, Watson: I am fully aware that it is neither a hansom nor yet the third to make its appearance. All rules, my dear Watson, were made to be broken, and time is of the essence.'

I consulted my hunter. He perceived my action though it was subtle of execution.

'I know we have two hours before we consult with Forrage but I believe I indicated that we might yet add to that reputation which I felt yesterday we were set to redeem.'

He ordered the cabdriver to turn into Leather Lane and to stop near a side entrance to Forrage's. He entered the store briskly and forgoing the lift he led the way up the stone steps which rather contrasted with the luxury of the rest of the store. Most people used the lifts or central staircases, which were of course extremely inviting. We reached his goal, the pet department, where he espied and gesticulated in the direction of that department's manager, steering him towards the aquarium tanks. He said, 'Grab a small net from the display, Watson, we may need it.'

The bemused manager blinked in disbelief as Holmes plied the tiny handling net among the silvery little fish in the first display tank. The net resurfaced, containing a small fish, even smaller than the others, but with angry red about its head and front swimming fins. He snapped at the manager, 'Fetch a fishbowl, man, with some water, for we need the evidence.'

The manager did as Holmes bade him and soon the detective had delved into most of the tanks and had collected fully half a dozen of the fiery little specimens. He suggested that the tanks should then be checked for dead or dying fish. After five minutes the man had made careful inspection and had discovered only a single fatality and only two wounded fish. It was considered that the wounded fish would recover and the manager was about to dispose of the mangled silvery corpse when my friend restrained him.

'My dear sir, kindly place it in a small

container. One of those intended to hold meal worms would do. Oh, and please place the swimming wounded into a bowl that I may take them to show Forrage. Tell me, sir, has anyone lingered near the tanks in any sort of suspicious manner this morning?'

'No, sir, and in fact I have had very few people in here today. I would have noticed any interference.'

Holmes pondered. 'So the introduction was possibly made last night.'

I asked, 'How can you account for so little damage having occurred if the sticklebacks had been here all night?'

'I imagine, Watson, that the tanks being in darkness saved the bulk of the fish from being attacked. It needed light, and a certain amount of heat generated by the lights over the tanks to enliven the evil little ides! We came here in the nick of time.'

As we made our way to Forrage's office, complete with fish bowls and meal worm case, I opened and shut my mouth a time or two, wishing to ask my friend a question but frightened that the answer would be so simple as to make me appear foolish. However, as so often in the past, Holmes raised the very point before I had dared to.

'Does it occur to you, Watson, that there is one element to all this which makes little sense? The message told us to 'BEWARE THE IDES OF MARCH'. Yet we are at the end of November, and the sticklebacks are wearing their spring coloration and showing the ferocity which they only display at that season.'

I did not admit to having had similar questions in mind because I felt that it might sound a little unconvincing. So instead I suggested, 'Could these fellows be of tropical origin, perhaps from the antipodes where the climates are reversed?'

He shook his head. 'I seem to remember that there are only two varieties of stickleback native to these waters, and aside from the mainland of Europe I do not believe they occur elsewhere. There are the three-spined and the twelve-spined varieties. These specimens which we have 'arrested' are of the three-spined variety. Notice the way they attack even each other in the bowl: one has already expired from a mauling. They build a nest in the reeds you know, Watson, and in this ruddy condition will attack anything that moves. The parent fish usually expire when the young have safely left the nest. They rely as a species upon a very fast replacement rate.'

We were early for our appointment with 'A.W.' and he emerged from his office, angry that we had interrupted a meeting of his stockholders.

'They have got some whiff of the troubles, Holmes, especially that concerning the elephant. I tell you, if any of this gets to the reporters of news I could be ruined. Well, what is it that makes you interrupt my meeting ... we said midday.'

Holmes explained the events of the morning, how he had deduced what were in fact the ides of March, and had anticipated how and where in the store they might do great damage. He showed the surviving fish in the bowl and the injured domestic stock. Then he opened the box and showed the grisly, mangled minnow.

Forrage started. There was a begrudging tone of admiration in his voice as he said, 'Bless my soul, you worked all that out, and managed to save the greater number of our pet fish? Only three affected among hundreds. Upon my word, Holmes, you are a shrewd fellow. Let me soothe these savage beasts and I will confer with you further.'

We retreated to one of the cafés for a light snack of coffee and rolls. Holmes had a glint of excitement in his eyes as he said, 'My dear Watson, things begin to fall into place. I will not spoil the game for you, for very soon all will become clear to your brain. But one thing I will tell you, one thing I will dare to predict; there will be another message from our foes before the day is out.'

The news that proved Holmes's prediction to be correct occurred even sooner I imagine than even he expected. As we went into Forrage's office he was standing with his back to us, hands held together behind that broad back, peering out at the London skyline. The boardroom table which had been set up in the apartment had not as yet been removed and Forrage wheeled around to face us and lifted a blotter at one of the set places. His action revealed one of those folded pieces of paper which were becoming so familiar. The store magnate snapped out, 'Look at that, Holmes, another of the blighters!'

Holmes seated himself in the chair where the note lay on the table. He opened the note carefully and read aloud, 'THE IVORIES MAY BLEED. Mr Forrage, when did you discover this note?'

'At the end of the meeting, when all but I had left. I tell you, Holmes, they are, several of them, on the point of putting their shares on the market at a loss. I tried to reassure them, but they were very grim, all of them. My last chance to rally them to my cause will be at my country house this weekend. All the shareholders, there are only six of them besides myself, I have invited to a house party. But what do you make of this latest curt threat?'

My friend considered, then replied, 'It could refer to the ivories in your fine arts department. Let us make our way there and see if anything seems amiss.'

Forrage's fine arts department has long been famous among collectors of the beautiful carved ivories, almost mass-produced in the Far East. I had so often admired those carved orbs, hollow and containing perhaps another such sphere. Then there were the figures of mandarins and rajahs ranging from a few inches high to life size. The staff, very grovelling in their manner, though perhaps mainly on account of the presence of 'A.W.', hovered around us as if competing to do our bidding. Forrage plainly disliked them and found this hard to conceal. 'Anything amiss in here, Warburton?'

'Oh no, sir, no, Mr Forrage. Everything is running as if on oiled tracks. Business is good too.'

'Well, check all the ivories . . . '

'I did that earlier, sir. Dusted them all, checked for any possible damage, and found everything shipshape and Bristol fashion, sir.'

'Well, check them all again, just do what I tell you, and send a boy to my office if you notice anything at all unusual here. Guard those ivories!'

We left fine arts and Forrage strode off impatiently, throwing a few passing words at us over his shoulder. 'Report back to me, Holmes, if you will, before you leave.'

We sauntered around fine arts for a while, looking at the pictures but always with half an eye upon the ivories. After an interval of about ten minutes the slimy Warburton sidled up to us and asked, 'Anything in particular you are seeking, gentlemen? We've got some splendid Landseer's and a cartoon by a French artist, Lautrec. Friends of dear Mr Forrage, are you, eh?'

He was so subservient that he seemed almost about to turn his frock-coated person inside out. I replied, 'Just acquaintances really, having a look round you know.'

He became a shade less obsequious. 'But you'll be going to his house party though, I'll wager?'

Holmes just about managed to conceal his dislike of this tiresome hireling. 'Very unlikely I would imagine.'

'Ooh!' Warburton put into this one elongated word a certain mixture of surprise and mild distaste. We were no longer to be fawned upon if we were not close enough to A. W. Forrage to be invited to his house party. He changed the subject. 'Of course, if it were not this particular time of year and if the old man was not on the prowl, my friend Horace and I would be going up to the music room to hear the recital, isn't that so, Horace?'

Another similarly clad and of like manner minced over to Warburton's side. He was even more slimy than his manager. 'Oh yes, I enjoy a good piano recital in the music room. You don't get, you know, common people at those.'

'A piano recital . . . where is the music room?'

I was a little surprised at the speed with which I found myself suddenly on my way to a recital, and in Forrage's of all places. However, I mused, if there is a circus, who knows what might be partially hidden within the big store's precincts. We seated ourselves in two chairs at the front of about fifty of them which had been arranged in front of a small dais upon which stood a Broadwood grand. A few more people eventually followed our example. There were perhaps thirty others seated beside ourselves when the musician mounted the dais. He was in full evening dress despite the early hour, and bowed to a smattering of applause. He said, 'Ladies and gentlemen, for my first piece I will play Rachmaninoff's *Prelude in C Sharp Minor*. Thank you . . . '

As he backed towards the piano he threw back a mane of reddish hair and made to sit upon the stool. Once seated he started to fiddle with his cuffs and waggle his fingers. Then he held both hands aloft as if to bring his fingers crashing onto the keys. Like many a pianist before him he imitated Paderewski's hesitance in bringing his hands down upon the keys. This hesitance saved him from a tragedy which to a pianist would be considered the most terrible of all.

Holmes suddenly leapt to his feet and shouted, 'Stop!'

The pianist sat there, an expression of

disbelief upon his face, his hands still poised above the keys. Holmes ran to him and grasped him by the wrists, shouting, 'Step aside man, or you will ever regret it.'

The pianist stood sheepishly aside and Holmes seated himself upon the stool. He gingerly placed a long slim forefinger upon one of the ivory keys. He depressed it so slowly and experimentally that it scarcely made a sound. He tried it again with others, and then found what he was seeking. I was at his shoulder as he showed me what he had discovered, and in the very nick of time.

'You see, Watson, there are wafer-thin blades of sharpened metal placed between certain keys which when depressed would have caused severe wounding to the pianist's fingers. As we sat, waiting for the first note I remembered hearing an expression to the effect that a pianist would 'tinkle the ivories'. A slang term, but it suddenly occurred to me that these could have been the ivories referred to in the latest threatening message.'

Thus Sherlock Holmes's ability to

retain the trivial in his mind and turn it to as much advantage as scientific data had saved the hands of a pianist: his most valuable asset saved. He was full of gratitude as he introduced himself. 'Sir, as you doubtless know, I am Lionel Fairburn, and might I know to whom I owe such a debt of gratitude?'

But I took my cue from Holmes that we were to remain anonymous. He shrugged off the pianist's gratitude, though politely, and we returned to confer with Forrage who was amazed and relieved by turns; but as ever did not show any great display of gratitude. He said, 'I see, so it was just luck, Holmes, that you were in the right place at the right time and had this sudden presentiment. Well, I suppose we must offer gratitude to providence. This settles it: you will both join my house party for the coming weekend. I would feel more comfortable if you were there, Holmes, in case you should have more bright anticipations.'

Holmes's eyes blazed but he remained calm, eventually saying, 'Who could refuse such a delightfully worded invitation?'

Forrage reacted with a glare, which melted as he thought better of the retort that I have no doubt he first intended. Instead he said, 'Oh, yes, quite, but I should have added that it will be a pleasure to have the company of yourself and the good Doctor. Dinner on Friday night, bit of a get together after, with my fellows of the board and, of course, their wives . . . so you will need to bring your tails rather than just dinner jackets. Oh, and bring your hunting togs as well, for we are holding a meet on Saturday.'

We dined back at Baker Street, having missed luncheon entirely so I was as hungry as the proverbial red-coated rider. This fact reminded me regarding the details of our invitation for the weekend. I remarked upon the sartorial instructions. 'Forrage must think that we are a real pair of oafs if he thinks that we would take dinner jackets to an affair where ladies will be present.'

'A self-made man, Watson. He poses as a lord of the manor, but were he the real thing he would not mention such details. By the way, do you have any hunting clothes? You know, of course, that I do not hunt.'

'Why yes, I believe I still have the necessary clothes and accessories somewhere, though I have not had occasion to use them for many years. But I fancy they will pass muster.'

6

The Wilde Quotation

Henley Grange proved to be a stately home that had been well maintained. The neatly raked gravel of its drive and the gleaming new paint upon its doors and window frames showed in contrast to most homes of this kind that I had seen. Baskerville Hall, for example, where tragedy there had been, but no shortage of funds had existed, had presented a certain stately weather-beaten aspect, as if no need existed to create an impression upon anyone. But Forrage's home, a splendid edifice built, I would hazard a guess, during the time of George the Second, seemed to gleam in a manner which shouted 'nouveau riche'. It was splendidly furnished and there were large oil portraits upon the staircase in the manner of an aristocratic residence. It was rather as if Forrage had purchased a set of ancestors along with his splendid house. There was a stable yard where his ostlers and grooms tended the carriage horses of his visitors, and beyond that a barn in which was housed our host's own vehicle, a gleaming Mercedes motor car with the name 'A. W. Forrage' painted upon each passenger door. The baying of hounds could be heard though the dogs could not be seen, but these sounds betrayed that Forrage kept his own pack.

As soon as we had arrived, late in the evening of Friday, Forrage himself met us at the door which a footman had opened, and he waved aside the looming, portly butler. 'Leave us, Higgs, I want to speak privately to these gentlemen. If I'm needed I will be in the library. But only if it is urgent.'

The library was splendid with its rows of beautifully leather-bound volumes. Holmes glanced at these and said, 'When you purchased this mansion, Forrage, I note that you took on all of its trappings save the books in this library. I see that despite their quality they are not of an age to match that which we espied in the hall and corridors. Notice, Watson, that the bindings fairly gleam with modernity.'

Forrage was gruff. 'How do you know that I did not take on a library and have all the volumes rebound?'

Holmes reached up and removed a book from its shelf. 'H. G. Wells? I notice also a set of Rudyard Kipling, perhaps too recent to require rebinding or to have been more than a decade in your hands.'

Forrage grunted. 'You have made your point, Holmes. I took on a furnished house from Lord Porting, but with a bookless library . . . the only things the poor old codger could not bear to part with. Well, a library usually grows, but I am a busy man with little time for reading, let alone browsing about in bookshops. I sent Higgs to the nearest bookshop with a couple of hundred pounds. First, of course, I had the shelves measured so that the right number of volumes could be purchased.'

Secretly I thought that I had never before heard of books being purchased by the yard. I observed that Forrage was impatient and uneasy. We were soon to learn why.

'I say, look here, there has been another of these beastly notes, but this time it has arrived here instead of at Forrage's! Can't even get away from it all at the weekend at my retreat. Not a word of this, Holmes; if the other shareholders get to know of this I really will be finished. Shares in Forrage's have already dropped dangerously. Look at this, man!'

He pointed dramatically to a fast becoming familiar sight, a white folded piece of paper. It lay upon his library table. Holmes made no movement so I examined it and read aloud the message, as usual neatly typed in capital letters:

PROTECT THE UNEATABLE

I added, 'Don't tell me he is threatening to poison your guests? I cannot quite think of any other connection to the word 'uneatable'. What do you make of it, Holmes?'

My friend examined the note carefully and then said, 'The infamous Oscar Wilde once referred to a fox hunt as 'The unspeakable in pursuit of the uneatable'. Obviously he makes some reference to your meet which I understand will be held upon the morrow. But I note something else that is significant. There is no threat implied, he simply suggests that you protect the fox. Further, I have noted with interest that the past few notes have dropped any suggestion of bribe or ransom being paid. This is rather strange. Well, it would be fairly easy for you to avoid any trouble implied by this note; you need only cancel your fox hunt. Leave pursuit of the 'uneatable' for another time and leave Reynard in peace.'

Forrage had shot Holmes several sharp glances as he spoke. But he only said, 'I cannot do that, I would be a laughing stock locally, especially if the reason for postponement were ever learned. As for my guests, they must not get a breath of any sort of threat or they would wonder why I would take such a step. What possible excuse could I give to call off?'

I put my word in. 'Could you not say that there was an outbreak of distemper among your hounds?'

Forrage retorted, 'Everybody knows that my pack is kept and tended far too carefully for that to happen. No, I will not disappoint my guests or make myself a laughing stock in Henley. The hunt must proceed.'

Holmes shrugged and his voice implied that he had offered the only advice that he could. 'So be it then, my dear Forrage. I can only say that I will observe events with interest.'

Forrage's voice grew weary as he said, 'Yes, well you do that, and it wouldn't hurt if you were to get one of those presentiments of yours.'

We left Forrage in his library to supervise the removal of our baggage to our rooms, which were upon the second of the two floors above. The servants were also housed on that floor and I remarked upon this to Holmes who replied, 'How apt, Watson, for I am indeed a servant, as you are yourself. I serve them when they lose a friend or relative or some valuable through foul play. As for yourself, you serve the public too, when they tire of ruining their health through over-indulgence or accident.'

He was right, of course, and perhaps one should never take offence at being so considered. I returned to the subject of the business in hand, seating myself upon Holmes's bed as he hung his clothes. I left my own unpacking until later. We had both refused the offer of a valet's services.

'What do you think about this latest note being delivered here instead of at Forrage's?'

Holmes replied, 'Well, doing so presents no particular problems for our quarry. Forrage's home address is no secret, having been the subject of a magazine article recently. But I think a word with Higgs before dinner might be in order. Speaking of which, you had better get about your sartorial business, Watson.'

He set about laying out out his dress clothes and patent boots as I left him to do the same. I dressed hastily, and when the dinner gong was heard I emerged to throw a hastening word over my shoulder as I made to descend the stairs. But I saw no sign of Holmes until he appeared a little later at the dinner table. He whispered, 'Higgs saw no one deliver the note, which of course he says he did not take to Forrage himself. He infers that his master discovered it upon the library table.'

The other guests, stockholders and their elegantly clad ladies, comfortably surrounded a not over large dining table. The silver cruets, decanters, trays and napkin rings were all engraved with the initials of the nobleman who had been the late owner of Henley Grange. The meal was extremely lavish, as was the circulation of wines and spirits during and after. There was a pause between the soup and the savoury during which Forrage addressed the company present, saying, 'Ladies and gentlemen, I wish you to meet that eminent detective, Sherlock Holmes. By the way the gentleman with the walrus moustache is none other than his friend and colleague, Dr John Watson. I thought I'd make the introduction: Holmes and Watson are not here in their professional capacities of course. But you know I always like to have something or someone interesting at my house parties. Let me take this opportunity to remind you of the meet tomorrow morning. Since the local hunt was discontinued, I have started one of my own. Never a dull moment at Forrage's, what?'

There were polite 'bravos' and muttered encouragements. The diner upon Holmes's left introduced himself, 'George Thompson, how d'ye do, gentlemen? Old Forrage says that you are here for pleasure rather than business, but I think he should engage you to enquire into the continued downward path that the jolly old Forrage's shares are taking. Thinking of selling mine, at a loss of course, before they hit rock bottom. Can't understand it; they usually go sky high at this time of the year. But the retail trade is a funny old game, it only takes a whisper in the market to start a decline.'

Thompson was not the only one to express such sentiments. Sir Hubert Carding had much the same to say when we were introduced to him later and were out of Forrage's earshot. He enlarged upon the theme slightly. 'You know there is some kind of rumour going about concerning Forrage's, as if someone knows that there is going to be a tragedy at the big store. Old man Forrage is looking a bit peaky too, don't you think? It's as if he knows what it is all about. I am doing what I can, but I am seriously thinking of putting my shares on the market. Now you are a shrewd man: young Baskerville fairly sings your praises. What would you do if you had shares in Forrage's?'

Holmes was as ever a master of diplomacy, at least when he chose to be. 'I would be alert, but be sure not to jump the gun. Rumour is a lying jade, please remember that.'

Sir Hubert looked thoughtful, then winked at Holmes and nudged me as he wandered off to circulate. When he was gone, I said, 'He seems to be voicing the general feeling of unrest. It would only take a breath of this latest threat concerning the fox hunt to set the cat among the pigeons. Pity you do not ride, Holmes, but rest assured, I will keep my eyes open at the meet.'

My friend replied, 'Oh, I ride well enough, Watson, it is just that hunting does not interest me, even this one, save where its itinerary may involve our interests. As you say, you will be my eyes and ears, but I will not be entirely outside the frame. Speaking of riding, I fancy a canter this very moment. Keep the flag flying, whilst I take one by moonlight on the safest horse I can find.'

I would have liked to accompany Holmes upon this unexpected moonlight ride, but realised that he wished me to remain and keep the flag flying. I felt sure that his forthcoming equestrian activity was no mere whim.

'Watson, where's Holmes?' It was Forrage who later made this enquiry. I told him that my friend had decided to take a stroll around the grounds. He was surprised though not deeply concerned, just mildly irritated. 'What am I paying the fellow for? I wanted him to circulate among my guests, to keep their minds off the dashed shares. Nothing like a celebrity to take the thoughts away from business. Not even taking part in the meet tomorrow either, even after he made some sort of translation of that beastly note to the effect that the hunt was threatened. Don't understand what Holmes is playing at, Watson.'

I said, 'Rest assured, Mr Forrage, that Holmes has your best interests at heart. I have never known him to indulge himself in seeking his own pleasures during an investigation. If I know him, he is at this moment smoking his pipe, deep in thought. I believe you can continue to trust the man who has already frustrated your enemies two or three times.'

Forrage grunted, but left me to my own devices as he wandered off to attend to his guests. I confess that at that particular moment I did indeed wonder just what Holmes was up to, why he was out riding, and yet preferred to be thought to be taking a stroll. After circulating for a while myself, I decided that I should try to earn my corn, so to speak, and determined to do a little investigating on my own account. Accordingly I took myself off to the entrance hall and lit a cigar.

Whilst doing so, I spied the butler, Higgs, who although not exactly having a quiet smoke himself, nevertheless gave the distinct impression of having absented himself from the proceedings in order to take a short rest.

I went up to Higgs, and asked him, 'Mr Forrage has, I think, already asked you about a note he received earlier?'

Higgs looked surprised, but nodded, wordlessly.

'Nothing to add to what you told him, have you?'

'No, sir.' He hesitated, 'I fear I scarcely follow you.'

I tried again. 'At what o'clock did Mr Forrage arrive at Henley Grange today?'

His look of surprise deepened, but he replied, 'Around four, sir.'

'I see. He left the store early, of course, to greet his guests. At what hour does he normally return, on a weekday, that is?'

'Around nine, sir.'

'I see,' I said again. Then I frowned, for here was an inconsistency which even Holmes had failed to spot. 'The store closes at six, though, does it not?'

'I believe so, sir,' said Higgs.

'But Mr Forrage has a new Mercedes!' I pointed out. 'It can surely not take him three hours to drive down here?'

'By no means, Dr Watson, but Mr Forrage's habit is to spend between half an hour and an hour in a thorough inspection of the store when all the staff have departed, and before the night-watchman arrives.'

'Oh? Odd, that?'

Higgs frowned. 'Mr Forrage is a very thorough, painstaking gentleman, sir. I understand that there was once a small fire at Forrage's which broke out when the staff had gone and before the night-watchman had arrived. Mr Forrage very naturally wishes to avoid a repetition of so unfortunate an occurrence.'

'H'mm.' Then, thinking that perhaps this mysterious fire might be connected with the equally mysterious threatening letters, I asked, 'When was that? And was the cause of the fire ever discovered?'

Higgs thought. 'It was several years back, sir. The cause was, I am given to understand, the failure — the 'shorting', I think the man said — of one of the new electric fittings which had just then replaced the old gas lights.'

'I see. Still, it rather smacks of keeping a dog and barking oneself, does it not?'

Higgs looked blank. 'Sir?'

I elaborated. 'If it were me, I should have the night-watchman start an hour earlier, instead of wandering round the store myself!'

'That was done at first, sir. But recently Mr Forrage changed things so that he himself checked the store. As I say, he is very thorough.'

'H'mm. And he is also alone in the store for an hour every evening?'

Higgs frowned, but nodded.

I decided that I was perhaps pursuing the subject too far, and indeed for the moment had forgotten the purpose of my original question. Fortunately I remembered and asked, 'By the way, was the note which Mr Forrage received delivered by hand?'

'No, sir, he discovered it in the library when he went in there.'

'Who do you suppose left it there?'

'I have no idea, sir. I was in the vicinity for quite a long time, and it was not there when I gave the room a last-minute check to be sure the ashtrays were clean and so on. That was about half an hour before Mr Forrage arrived. Will that be all, sir?'

I nodded, 'Thank you, Higgs, do not let me detain you.'

The butler bowed politely and went about his duties. I considered what I had learned. I wondered why Holmes had not thought to make such enquiries, but decided that he might have learned these things from another source and thought them too unimportant to impart.

* * *

One of the big reception rooms had been cleared for dancing, with a small platform at one end where the musicians from Forrage's tea lounge had been installed. They played a series of waltz, gavot and polka for the pleasure of the dozen or so rather ponderous dancers. I realised that it would be difficult for me to avoid altogether dancing with one or two of the ladies who had husbands disinclined or unable to dance. To the strains of *The Blue Danube* I waltzed around the floor with a Lady Grundy-Smythe, an ample lady with extremely large feet. She wheezed at the effort of dancing and confided to me, 'We've all got shares in Forrage's, y'know; at least my husband has, and I suppose so have these others.'

She waved her closed fan in the general direction of other dancers, managing to give the gesture a somewhat dismissive touch. Then she continued, 'The shares have gone down, you know, and I've advised Bertie to sell before it all ends in tears. But there, it's only a few thousand.'

I soon realised that Forrage got full value from his staff, for in addition to the musicians already mentioned, an interlude occurred when we were entertained by 'Professor Stanley Collins', the expert demonstrator from Forrage's conjuring department. I already knew what a clever conjurer he was, but a demonstration is not always the same as an entertainment. Here the dynamic young man extracted real half-crowns from the air, from his elbow, from the sole of his pump and from the ears of spectators. As he caught each eye-catching silver coin he deposited it onto a saucer which he had placed inside his opera hat. As each coin dropped to make a satisfying 'clink' the conjurer made a comical remark. He finished with the coins by producing a final shower of them, causing them to cascade from his hand to the saucer. Next he performed with playing cards, making the four aces assemble together in a shuffled pack, causing selected paste-boards to rise up out of the pack when it was isolated in a glass tumbler, and to conclude a spirited performance he caused a tiny replica of a selected card to appear inside the cover of my hunter!

Then, 'direct from Maskelyne's theatre' rather than any department of Forrage's, there appeared a ventriloquist, one 'Nelson Hardy', who appeared to throw his voice so that it seemed a pedler was selling his wares immediately outside the big bay window. One spectator was suspicious enough to run outside the building to ensure himself that a confederate was not providing the pedler's voice! Then Mr Hardy took upon his knee a lay figure in a sailor suit, with a red-wigged, cheeky head and moving jaw. This doll appeared to take on a life of its own and continued to speak in a voice quite unlike that of Mr Hardy, even when that ventriloquist drank water and smoked a cigarette. The cheeky puppet made quite personal remarks concerning some of the company present, evidently annoying his master as much as those he tormented.

After this modest but stylish entertainment had concluded, I was beginning to wonder just when and where Sherlock Holmes would make his reappearance. Then quite suddenly he was there, in animated conversation with another of the shareholders, Lord Preston. I wandered over to join him and in a manner very irritating and typical of him, Holmes asked me, 'Where on earth have you been all evening, Watson? The last I saw of you was when you took to the floor with Lady Grundy-Smythe after which you seemed to disappear.'

I was furious, thinking that he had actually remained present in the shadows, or that he had been enquiring of my activities among the guests. But later, when the company had all taken to their beds and we sat before the roaring fire, he said, 'My dear fellow, you must not be too hard on me for saying what I did; I was merely trying to keep up the pretence of having been present the whole time. Forrage's guests are not over-endowed with alertness.'

'You mean you really did go off on that excursion of yours?'

'I certainly did and very enlightening it was.'

'Who then told you that I danced with Lady Grundy-Smythe, or even that I danced at all?'

'No one, it was elementary. That you had been dancing I could see from the trace of french chalk on the toe of your right pump; that and the white glove protruding from your coat-tail pocket. That it was the lady I named was obvious because she is the only lady who was present of a height to correspond with the slight trace of cosmetic powder that decorates the right shoulder of your dress coat.'

Of course it all made perfect sense. Lady Grundy-Smythe was perhaps five feet and three; the other ladies present being all of five feet and seven or even more. He was right too about the french chalk and the dress glove; it was all 'elementary', but only when Sherlock Holmes had explained it.

I marvelled that Holmes, ever the perfectionist, had taken such pains to change back into his evening clothes from those that he must have used to ride. But more, he had made sure to trail a paper streamer over one shoulder as if he had indeed been at the centre of festivities. Yet I well knew that he had not, and was anxious to hear of his adventures. However, I knew of old that Sherlock Holmes would not be rushed into the revelations that he could present. At last, however, having finished filling his pipe and lighting it from a brand from the fire, he began his narration.

'Having attired myself suitably, I went

to the stables and asked the groom to prepare me a mount. When he made to bring forth a jaunty gelding which might have tripped from excitement, let alone accident, I reproved him, saying, 'Pray find me a solid mount such as you might ride across wild country and find dependable and with more common sense than temperament.' He said, 'Ah, then if appearance does not matter, I'll bring out old Plodder.' I liked the name, and the mount itself, it being a short-legged fellow, more like a large pony than a small horse. I reckoned that he had some Exmoor in him and was as steady as a rock.

'My plan was to take him round the jumps which I knew would figure in the hunt, but intended to give him his head so that he would take them at his own speed and could refuse them should he decide to do so.'

I threw in an observation at this point. 'You endow the horse in your mind with more intellect than do the scientists, who place it well down the scale. I have heard of a jockey walking the course before a race, but not in partnership with a horse.'

'Your scientific colleagues may be right concerning the thoroughbred, Watson, but your Exmoor, Dartmoor or fells pony is a different creature, from a wild background where one slip upon a moor may mean death through falling from a crag or drowning in a bog. Anyway, I trusted Plodder and he took me over the jumps, slowly and carefully. He had obviously followed the course before, yet took nothing for granted. The first few jumps were easy for him, as also was a copse through which he showed no hesitation. But then when we came to the spaced out, higher stiles and leaps he became wary as I had trusted him to. Eventually he refused a jump which took the form of a gate fixed between two trees. I encouraged him, even speaking sharply, but he still refused the jump. I dismounted and examined the gate which proved firm and unremarkable. Then I walked around to its far side and discovered that there was a large puddle of water. Probing with a stick revealed that there were potholes and irregularities beneath the muddy water which would surely prove treacherous to any horse attempting to land its front feet therein. Certain unsaddling and possibly even serious injury for both rider and mount.'

I was aghast. 'Shall you at once inform Forrage?'

He waved this suggestion aside. 'No need, Watson, for I have made the jump safe by pulling strong saplings over the defects to make a safe landing for any horse. I showed the pony what I had done and then took him over it safely. The remainder of the jumps presented no problems. Then the tracks across open country were obviously a safe ride. I shall tell no one of my findings, and reactions to the safe clearance of the dangerous jump by the leading rider should be interesting. Watson, I wish you to keep up tomorrow and observe any show of surprise.'

'You are determined not to ride yourself then still?'

'Quite so, but I will watch through binoculars from a copse towards the end of the course, in case our adversary has some other surprise in store.'

Despite the lateness of the hour we continued to sit by the huge fire until it had burned down and we had exhausted the logs that had been left. We discussed at length for the first time all possibilities and suspects that could thus far have presented themselves to us. The reader might suppose from my presentation of the facts that we had no actual suspects in mind, but this was not so for I had suspected perhaps a dozen persons in their turn. Holmes had probably considered less than that number as suspicious through the process of logical elimination. But at this point I will admit that I had suspected all of the department managers with whom we had come into contact, and all of Forrage's fellow shareholders.

When I mentioned them to Holmes he said, 'Watson, you suspect all of these people without any really substantial evidence. You have suspected them in turn because they all have one thing in common: a guarded, and in some cases disguised, hatred for Forrage himself. Yet they cannot all be guilty save through a monster of a conspiracy. Remember this, Watson, they share a rather general feeling experienced by all who are close to or employed by Forrage. He is popular only with the general public who know him only as the provider of inexpensive glories and Yuletide cheer. He is not a man easy to tolerate, let alone like. So your suspects will have to possess more than a mere dislike.'

I cut my mental list of suspected persons to those whom I felt had opportunity, as he felt that aversion was not enough. I said, 'The manager of the stationery and office accessories has access to a battery of brand-new Remingtons. Enough that he could have typed those notes upon a fresh one each time.'

Holmes nodded. 'I had, of course, considered that, also the fact that a brand-new ribbon would have to be fitted to the machine used and the old one disposed of. I have not entirely dismissed him from my mind.'

I considered. 'How about the manager of the conjuring department?'

'I have no reason to suspect him save the very nature of his profession, Watson.'

'The livestock manager could have introduced those ferocious little fish himself.'

Holmes shrugged, 'Perhaps the music administrator also arranged for those steel blades to be inserted between the keys of the piano, just after he had finished typing the threat in the business supplies section? No, Watson, I have carefully considered all of these possibilities and soon came to the conclusion that I was on the wrong track. These people are obvious suspects, yet we are dealing with a wily adversary.'

By now the fire was low enough to make the room chilly. No logs remained and I had not the cruelty in my heart to ring the bell which might bring a pyjama-clad footman. Instead I said, 'Well, Holmes, perhaps the morrow will furnish you with fresh food for thought.'

7

The Henley Hounds

It was a fine late November morning, cold but dry, that dawned on the Saturday. Privately I thought it a trifle early in the season for anything in the nature of a great run, but at Henley Grange all efforts were being made to ensure the success of the hunt. Ostlers and grooms were busy with their equine charges, making them presentable and ensuring that they were in top condition for the chase.

It was a traditional enough scene outside the Fox and Hounds as we sat outside that ancient hostelry, accepting glasses of sloe gin or brandy from the buxom barmaid.

Or most of us did; somewhat reluctantly I refused the proffered tray, thinking it as well to keep a clear head. I nudged my horse away from the crowd, and took a look at the country round about. It was thickly wooded in places, no chance of a gallop there, but still there were plenty of fields and meadows — and plenty of fences and gates! Even granted that old Dobbin, or Plodder, or whatever he was called, had hunted the country for many years and knew all the most likely runs, Holmes must have had his work cut out to check each and every possible jump! I smiled at the thought, and then frowned as a more serious thought occurred to me. Suppose Holmes had not checked every jump? Suppose our mysterious enemy had sabotaged not one, but two or more, of the fences and gates? I had not thought to bring my medical bag along with me, but I did take the precaution of asking the barmaid to fill my flask, which might perhaps be needed after all.

As I was tucking the flask safely into my boot, Forrage rode up to me. 'No sign of Holmes, I see? I had hoped he might be on hand to prevent any — unpleasantness.' There was an odd note in his voice, which I half-believed was trepidation, if not actual fear. The notes and the incidents must, I reflected, have undermined even Forrage's iron will.

I made some non-committal remark as to Holmes having his own methods, and Forrage grunted as if to intimate that he was far from satisfied, but could do nothing at the moment. He nodded curtly, and urged his horse back to the field.

I had, in my innocence, expected that Forrage himself would lead the hunt, but the master was one Sir Hubert Carding, who was, I learned, the chairman of the board of directors of Forrage's. Sir Hubert certainly looked the part in his red coat and beaver hat. I suspected then, and I still think now, that Forrage had an accurate idea of his own abilities, and did not wish to make a spectacle of himself before the county, preferring to wait until he had acquired sufficient expertise before he ventured to take over the mastership. Be all that as it may, Forrage deferred to Sir Hubert very properly.

The huntsman blew his horn, and we set off. A few villagers had turned out to watch, and they cheered in a half-hearted fashion as we went past. I felt that it was more from a sense of obligation to Forrage, as their landlord or employer, than from any real enthusiasm; Forrage certainly inspired a kind of respect, perhaps even fear, in his underlings, but no real affection, thought I.

I have said that I thought it early for success, and so it proved. We found quickly, but the hounds lost the scent after a few moments, and the huntsman led us off to draw elsewhere. As I sat watching the hounds snuffling around, I became aware that, not too far away, was a curious sort of jump, a rickety old gate fixed between two old trees, evidently that jump which, on the previous evening, Holmes had found wanting and had repaired. I looked around, to see if I could spot Holmes, but if he were there he was well concealed, too well for me to see him.

There was a shout from someone or other, and I glanced round to spot the familiar streak of red-brown chasing away on the far side of the gate. Forrage himself was nearest the jump, and he was the first to go over it. And I must say that he took it in fine style, chasing after Charlie like a good 'un. Before I had properly realised what had happened, away went Charlie, away went Forrage, away went the rest of the field. I myself brought up the rear, reflecting that I had erred in not taking note of who amongst my fellow huntsmen showed any surprise that Forrage had not broken his neck. Still, I had not expected the sudden burst of activity — and if Holmes had been there, as he had said he would be, then he himself could have taken note! If I had been remiss, then so too had Holmes.

As before, the hounds lost the scent, and old Charlie lived to fight another day. I was not sorry — no true sportsman ever is, despite the sardonic mutterings of Oscar Wilde and his fellows, none of whom have ever actually followed the hunt, other than from an armchair!

We drew a few more coverts, with no success. The afternoon was drawing on, and the sun was now sinking behind a great bank of cloud. Sir Hubert conferred with his huntsman and his whips, and the proceedings came to an end.

As I changed before dinner, Holmes appeared suddenly and silently. He was clad in an old tweed suit, and carried a pair of field glasses. 'Ah, Watson. I trust you have a good appetite after the thrill of the chase?'

'I always do, Holmes! It was a grand day out, mind, as you would have seen had you carried out your intention and observed the day's sport.'

'I did, Watson.'

'Oh? I never saw you.'

Holmes smiled. 'That is what I intended, dear fellow. Nonetheless, I was there.' He frowned.

'And what did you see?'

'I confess that I did not see what I expected. Or, rather, I saw that which I did not expect to see.'

'And what was that?' I asked, puzzled.

'I saw our host take the jump first.'

'Oh?' I was more puzzled than ever. 'And why should — oh!'

Holmes nodded. 'Yes, a short interview after dinner with Mr Forrage is very definitely indicated, Watson, so keep yourself in readiness for that. Meantime, I must change, for the hour is later than one might think.' And not another word could I get out of him, despite all my questions.

I had my dinner, being quite literally as hungry as a hunter, though I could not begin to tell you just what the menu might have been, so eager was I to get more information from Holmes. I do recall that I drank only sparingly of our host's excellent wines, being mindful of Holmes's injunction to remain alert for the interview with Forrage.

When the meal was over and people were beginning to say goodnight, Holmes sought out Forrage, who ushered us into his private study. Our host seemed more than keen to express his own sentiments. 'Turned up, have you?' he began. 'Better late than never, I suppose! In the event, your services were not needed, for nothing untoward occurred. Still, you were not to know that. You ought to have been there, keeping an eye on things.'

'Oh, but I was,' said Holmes. 'I was

ensconced in a hedgerow in a corner of what I believe is called the Four Acre field. You know it?'

Forrage looked puzzled, but nodded. 'And what of it?'

'You took the gate there in fine fashion, once the 'view halloo' was given.'

'Again, what of that?'

'Did the jump not trouble you?'

Forrage looked more puzzled than ever. 'The landing was a bit soft, springy, now you mention it. But — '

'Would it interest you to know that there had been some meddling with the far side of that jump? That someone had dug a concealed pitfall that was intended to unseat any rider going over it? Unseat him, if not worse? I myself repaired the damage as best I could with brushwood, and that undoubtedly accounts for the softness that you noted on landing.'

For a long moment, Forrage said nothing, but the colour drained from his countenance. Then he gasped, 'But — !' and put a hand to his chest, as if he were in pain.

I stood up, thinking that my professional services might be urgently
required.

Forrage waved me away, stood up, and
helped himself to whisky, a generous
measure of the spirit with the merest
splash of soda. He gulped it down in one,
then remembered his manners and waved
a hand at the decanter. 'Can I — ?'

'Thank you, no,' said Holmes. As
Forrage poured a second drink for
himself, Holmes went on, 'This business
has gone on long enough, I think you will
agree, sir.'

'Oh, yes, indeed! More than long
enough, I quite agree,' said Forrage.
'Holmes — Mr Holmes — you must help
me! This note — these notes, that is to
say, you must find out who wrote it
— them.'

'As you say. It is, of course, the latest
note which is the real, the only, puzzle,'
said Holmes with a thin smile. 'We must
each do our part. I will undertake to do
mine, Mr Forrage — and you?'

Forrage nodded, wordlessly. He gulped
as if for air once or twice, then managed,

'It will be as you say. There will be no — that is, I — that is, it will be as you say.'

Holmes stood up, ignored the hand which Forrage offered him, and said, 'Do you have the latest note?'

'Why, yes.' Forrage opened a drawer of his desk, produced the note and handed it to Holmes.

'Thank you. Come, Watson, we have much to discuss.'

I stammered out a 'Good night' to the still distraught Forrage, and followed Holmes upstairs, determined not to let him rest until he had shared whatever he knew with me.

'Well, Watson,' said Holmes, taking out his cigar case and offering it to me. 'What is your reading of the matter thus far?'

'Forrage was certainly taken aback when you told him that he himself had been in danger of his life.'

'Yes?'

'And now I think about it, when he spoke of that latest note to me earlier, he did sound — different.'

'Different?' said Holmes, with a frown.

'Yes, different. He seemed genuinely worried by it, puzzled by it. And he had not seemed so with the earlier notes.' I thought a moment. 'Holmes?'

'Yes, Doctor?'

'Those earlier notes?'

'Yes?'

'I have a suspicion — no! It is too silly. But then again — look here, Holmes, did Forrage himself write those other notes?'

Holmes nodded. 'He did. Well done, Watson. He most likely used the new typewriting machines in his own store.'

'Of course he did. I learned the other day that he is in the habit of spending an hour or so alone in the store each evening after it closes.'

'Well done again, Watson! I had missed that, but it confirms things nicely.'

'But would the typewriter ribbons not show they had been used?'

'Oh, that is easy enough. He keeps a special ribbon for the purpose, most likely locked away in his safe. He winds it on each time to use a fresh section, so that the notes are all pristine. Will that serve?'

'It will.' I put a hand to my head, to try

to stop its spinning round. 'And the other things, the razor blades in the piano , the piranhas in the goldfish bowls? All Forrage's own handiwork?'

Holmes nodded again. 'His, or that of his agents.'

'But why? In the name of Heaven, why? The pianist might have been disfigured for life! And the elephant — that poor woman might have been crushed to death. Why, Holmes? What is at the back of it all?'

'To drive the share price down, of course.'

'But that would not benefit him! He is a major shareholder! Why, it is his own store!'

Holmes smiled. 'In name only, Watson. True, Forrage owns a large block of the shares, but he is by no means the only shareholder, or even a major shareholder. It must be galling for him to see his own name up on the shop front, to know that he himself built the store up more or less from a coster's barrow, and yet he is compelled to consult men whose only claim is that they have money to buy the shares! To consult them? Nay, to defer to them. Galling, and more than galling. True, his own holding is worth considerably less, thanks to the fall in the price of the shares, but he sustains a real loss only if he sells those shares. And he does not — or did not, rather — intend to sell. He intended to buy, to increase his holding at low cost, until he became the controlling shareholder, until he need not consult anyone or defer to anyone. My contacts tell me that someone has been buying the shares using agents, nominees. I have no doubt that Forrage is hiding behind those nominees, Watson. However, as you say, this latest business has unsettled him, and I think there will be no more from that quarter, at any rate.'

'But, Holmes! What of the poor people he has defrauded?'

He nodded. 'There will have to be some restitution, of course. An expensive business for Forrage, but that is his affair.'

'And then, Holmes, what of the latest note? If Forrage did not send that, who did?'

'Ah, there you have me, Doctor. That is

the remaining element of the puzzle, and the most interesting one.' He held up the note. 'I confess that I erred in not examining this more closely. But now that I do, I see that it is quite different from the others.' He handed it across to me, along with his powerful lens.

I made a pretence of studying the note. 'Very interesting — oh! Yes, Holmes, even I can see that the letter 'E' is worn at the bottom, so that it is almost an 'F'. An older machine has been used.'

Holmes nodded. 'There are six other indications, but that is the most obvious, 'e' being, as you are aware, the most widely used letter in English.'

I was warming to my task. 'And even then, the fact that the upper-case 'e' is worn indicates that the machine has indeed seen much use, for the lower case is normally used more than the upper.'

He positively beamed at me. 'The country air has done wonders for your powers of ratiocination, Watson.'

I ignored this. 'That still tells us very little. For example, given that Forrage was trying to drive the shares down, why has some third party, as it were, stepped in and sent this last note? Why try to kill Forrage?'

'That is surely obvious. Our mystery man observed that the shares were going down in consequence of the previous notes, and decided to make a little profit on his own account.'

'But he could hardly know that Forrage would be first over the fence!' I expostulated.

Holmes smiled. 'It was not necessary that Forrage should break his neck, Watson. It was merely necessary that our man should not! Were any of the major shareholders to be thus killed, whoever it might have been, the share price would undoubtedly have fallen yet further. City men are a superstitious lot, you know, and a tragedy today would have added to that air of desolation which already surrounds Forrage's shares. And if the heirs of the dead man had sold a large block of shares, at an already low price — well!' He sighed. 'We did very badly, I must say, Watson. Had I — or you, my dear fellow — been sufficiently alert, we might have seen who showed surprise at Forrage's not tumbling off his horse. But I was sure that it was Forrage, and so I was watching him.'

'You were right, though. It was Forrage, most of the time, so you can hardly blame yourself too much.'

'You are too kind, Watson. Still, I must now try to redeem myself by deducing what I can from this latest note.' He regarded me with a quizzical eye.

'I can't see that there is much to deduce,' said I ruefully. Feeling this was rather lame, I added, 'It must have been someone who could leave the note where Forrage would find it, of course. And he — our man, I mean — must have been here to fiddle with the jump — Holmes, he must be here! That is, he must be one of the guests here with us now!'

Holmes nodded. 'Of course he must. We already knew it must be a major shareholder, and they are all at Henley Grange, as you observe.'

'Well! Of course, one knew, in a theoretical way, so to speak, but still, it is hardly pleasant to think that one has just dined with a man who would not stop at murder!'

'It is as well for your appetite that you did not know this earlier, I agree,' said Holmes.

I ignored this slander. 'I suppose that if we could examine the machine that was used to write the note — but then it might be any machine.'

'Nay, for we have just deduced that the note was written by one of the guests here. A mere half-dozen machines to check.'

'Even so, Holmes, a man does not carry a typewriting machine around with him when he goes to a house party for the weekend! He clearly typed the note before he left home.' And before Holmes could speak, I added, 'No, he did not! He typed it at his office, of course!'

Holmes raised an eyebrow.

I told him, 'The worn upper-case 'e', Holmes. It is an office where they use the upper case for typing invoices and the like. It must be, to wear it so.'

He held out his hand. 'You scintillate, Watson.'

'You know my methods, Holmes. But I still cannot see how that helps, unless we break into each of their offices and check their typewriting machines!'

'That will be unnecessary, I fancy. Have you a pencil and paper there?'

'Of course, Holmes. I am a writer, after all. Oh, my pencil needs sharpening, though.'

'Then pray sharpen it,' said he, handing me his pocket knife. 'And take this down — 'Mr James Ellis begs the favour of a short interview with — ' and leave a blank there, Watson, which we shall fill up as required — 'and respectfully requests that a note of a suitable date and time might be sent as soon as practicable to him, care of 221B Baker Street'. That will meet the case, I think.'

'And who, pray, is Mr James Ellis? Oh, I see, it's to get a capital 'e', of course! If we said 'Ebenezer Ellis', that would give twice the evidence, you know.'

Holmes nodded. 'I shall write a half dozen notes, one to each of the business addresses of the guests here, and post them on my return to London. We shall be most unlucky indeed if none of the typewriters is the correct one.'

'The notes would look better typed, Holmes,' I said. 'Old Forrage probably has a typewriter here which I could borrow. I keep meaning to try one, but I've never had the nerve.'

He nodded. 'That would be a kindness, Watson. And we shall await the favour of a reply, as the business phrase has it, with keen anticipation.'

8

The Stockholders' Meeting

'It is most irregular, Mr Holmes!' said Sir Hubert Carding with some asperity.

'Sir Hubert, I was engaged by Mr Forrage to investigate a most disturbing sequence of events. Events,' said Holmes, sternly, 'which have led to financial loss for many small investors, and which might have led to outright tragedy.'

Sir Hubert was somewhat mollified. 'You say that you wish to address the board?'

Holmes nodded. 'Purely unofficially, of course. Before your formal proceedings begin.'

'And then to interview each one of us in turn?'

'Merely a short interview with each of you.'

'And the purpose of these interviews?' asked Sir Hubert.

'I have something to say to one of you.'

'Then why not simply talk to the man concerned?' Sir Hubert wanted to know.

'Because I do not wish to identify the man,' said Holmes calmly.

Sir Hubert shrugged his shoulders, and I fancy that I caught the words, 'damned nonsense!' or something very like them. But he said only, 'Very well, Mr Holmes. If that is your price for solving our little problem, so be it.'

He led us into the board room, where the directors were gathered round a great oval oak table. 'Mr Sherlock Holmes wishes to address us before we begin,' said Sir Hubert.

'Thank you,' said Holmes. He glanced around the table. 'You will be only too well aware that Forrage's has been somewhat troubled of late,' he began.

'Too true!' came from more than one of the listeners.

Holmes held up a hand and went on, 'I can promise you that the danger is past. Or at least,' he added, as there was a murmur at this, 'it will be past once I have had a private word with each and every one of you.' And he nodded, and stalked out of the room, with me at his heels, leaving some very puzzled men staring after him.

Forrage provided us with a little office, and the members of the board of directors, all major shareholders, trooped in one at a time. Forrage himself was the first to come in. He sat down, avoiding Holmes's eye. 'Solved it, have you?' he asked gruffly.

Holmes nodded. 'There must, of course, be restitution, reparation,' he said. 'Provided that is done, and provided that there is no repetition of this nonsense, then I can guarantee that all will be well. All will be hushed up, as it has so often in the past. Not for you,' he added, as Forrage made as if to say something, 'but for the smaller shareholders, those who have held on to their shares loyally through thick and thin. Were I to ruin you — and make no mistake, I could, and would, under different circumstances! — then they too would be ruined. And I have a soft spot, as Watson will tell you, for widows and orphans.'

Forrage stared at him, then nodded. 'Very well.' He hesitated. 'Er — this reparation of which you speak,' he added. 'What does that mean, exactly?'

'It means that you, or your agents, must sell back the shares you bought for the price you paid,' said Holmes.

Forrage put a hand to his forehead. 'But — how can I identify who sold the shares?'

'There are records, are there not?'

'True, but it will be an enormous task!'

'You should have thought of that,' said Holmes.

'An enormously expensive task! I shall be ruined.'

'You should have thought of that too! Regard it in the light of a penance, or fine for your misdemeanours,' said Holmes. 'At that it is better than seven years' hard labour.'

Forrage shuddered, then recovered himself somewhat. 'Ah, but what if they do not wish to buy the shares back?' he asked, a sly look creeping over his face.

'You will, of course, offer to sell at the current price — '

'But I'll take a massive loss!' cried Forrage.

Holmes stared him into silence. 'Seven years,' he mused, as if to himself. Then, to the now thoroughly crestfallen Forrage, 'And you will tell them that I, Sherlock Holmes, assure them that the trouble is over, that the shares should soon regain their former glory.'

Forrage groaned aloud. 'Seven years!' he muttered. 'It would almost be worth it!'

'Almost,' agreed Holmes, 'but not quite.'

Forrage put his head in his hands. 'Very well,' he said at last. 'I agree. But what of that last note? Who was the villain responsible for that?'

'You expect me to hush up your part in this affair,' said Holmes. 'You must accept that I shall extend the same discretion to the other man concerned.'

Forrage looked unhappy at this, but then reflected a moment, and nodded agreement. 'Mind you,' he complained, 'it's not a pleasant thought, to know that one of your fellow directors has been up to some hanky-panky!'

Coming from the instigator of the hanky-panky, I personally thought this was rich! But Holmes merely waved a hand to dismiss him. 'Send in Mr Grundy-Smythe, would you?'

Grundy-Smythe came in, and Holmes asked him a few questions about his shareholdings, receiving the rather shame-faced information that Grundy-Smythe had sold 'a few shares' recently, rather than face a heavy loss. Holmes reassured him that things would improve, and the rather disloyal director mumbled something to the effect that he would 'buy them back if he could.'

The other directors in turn came in, and Holmes talked to all of them much as he had talked to Grundy-Smythe. All, that is, until Sir Hubert himself came in last of all, and sat down.

'Well, Mr Holmes?'

'Well, Sir Hubert? How have you reacted to this fall in the price of Forrage's shares?'

Sir Hubert frowned. 'I don't quite follow you, Mr Holmes. I'm damned annoyed, if that is what you mean.'

'It was not quite what I was driving at, Sir Hubert. I meant rather to ask if you had sold any of your shares?'

'Far from it! I've been buying them, as many as I can afford. Partly to try to support the price, partly because I knew they would be a good investment in the long term. Bound to come back, once this nonsense is sorted out. And now you say it is sorted out, so there you are!' he concluded with an air of triumph.

I could tell that this was not what Holmes had expected. After a moment, he nodded. 'That is what I have learned,' he said, 'and I confess that I find it odd.'

Sir Hubert stared at him in evident astonishment. 'Odd that I should buy the firm's shares? Oh, I see, you mean because of the fall in the price? Well, Mr Holmes, firstly, as I have just told you, I regard that as a purely temporary setback, a golden opportunity to buy shares which are, at bottom, a solid investment, at a knock-down price. I am, after all, a businessman.'

'And secondly?' asked Holmes.

'Oh, there is a proverb about rats and sinking ships. Not that I'm calling any of my fellow directors rats, of course,' said Sir Hubert hastily. 'But I think one ought to support a firm in which one has shares, a firm of which one is chairman, don't you?'

Holmes looked baffled. He took a sheet of paper from his pocket book, and handed it over to Sir Hubert. 'That was typed on the machine in your own office in the City,' he told him.

Sir Hubert raised an eyebrow. He glanced at the note. 'It appears to be addressed to one Ebenezer Ellis, making an appointment for an interview,' said he. He handed the note back. 'I fear that the name is not immediately familiar to me.'

Holmes waved a hand. 'Be that as it may, do you deny that it was typed on your office machine?'

'Why the devil should I deny it? If you say it was. I'm happy to accept that such is the case. It is on my office notepaper, and it's signed by Mr Chapman, who is my office manager, so I dare say you are right. But I ask again, what of it?'

'And you do not deny buying Forrage's shares?'

Sir Hubert stood up. 'We have been through that. I think this interview is over, Mr Holmes, unless you have new questions to ask me?'

'Forgive me, Sir Hubert, but I confess I am puzzled. This note — ' and Holmes stared at the note. 'It is from your office, but — ' He shook his head. 'Tell me, Sir Hubert, would you know if any of your employees have bought shares in Forrage's?'

Sir Hubert sat down again. 'This is important, Mr Holmes? Of course it is, I know your reputation. Well, I do not know if any of my own employees have bought shares in Forrage's. But I should guess that if any of them had shares in this firm, they have probably sold them at a loss.'

'H'mm. The threatening notes, Sir Hubert, and the little incidents — did you discuss them with anyone, apart from your fellow directors, that is?'

'Hardly! After all, one would scarcely wish to add to the rumours that are

169

already circulating.'

'So you would not speak of it to your own employees? No, I see. Any information they had would be no more than was generally circulating. I confess it is a pretty puzzle.'

Sir Hubert regarded Holmes keenly. 'I see that you attach some considerable importance to all this, Mr Holmes, but I admit its significance escapes me. My own employees, as you say, knew nothing more of the matter than was known by all and sundry. And then why should I not buy Forrage's shares? As I say, at the lower price they were a good investment.' He laughed. 'I suppose now that everything is cleared up, I shall make a fair profit. Though I admit that I had half an eye to taking control of the firm, putting Herbert in as manager. The poor boy will be disappointed, but I expect he'll get over it.'

'Herbert?' asked Holmes, sitting up.

'Herbert Dawlish. My nephew. A good lad,' said Sir Hubert, his face clouding slightly. 'Though I'll not deny he has a way with him. You know him,' he added, 'if only sightly. He was at old Forrage's party at the weekend.'

I had a vague memory of a young man with an incipient moustache and a somewhat furtive air. Holmes, too, nodded as if recollecting young Herbert. 'Your nephew works for you, at Carding's?' he asked casually.

Sir Hubert nodded. 'Owed it to my sister,' he said. 'He's not the best of workers, but I have hopes for him. My nearest relative, now that my sister's dead. I never married or anything, so Herbert will inherit the lot.'

'I see.' Holmes stood up. 'Where is Herbert now?' he asked casually.

'Here at Forrage's, somewhere about the place. We're dining together after the board meeting, and meantime he's doing a bit of foraging, shopping and what have you. Help to swell the takings, you see?'

'Thank you,' said Holmes. 'We shall not detain you further, Sir Hubert. Please reiterate to the board what I said earlier, that things will mend from now. Come along, Watson.'

As he led the way downstairs, I said,

'Hubert and Herbert. Lack of imagination, there, Holmes. Sounds like a music-hall double act.'

'Indeed. Though perhaps not quite so amusing as might at first appear.' Holmes glanced round each floor as we went, pausing at gents' outfittings, and saying, 'That is young Herbert, if I am not mistaken?'

'It is,' said I.

Holmes went up to the young man, who was considering the merits of a tray of evening gloves. 'Mr Dawlish?'

'Guilty.' He looked a question.

'My name is Sherlock Holmes, and this is Dr John Watson.'

'Ah.'

'I see you have heard of us.'

Dawlish nodded towards the coffee lounge. 'Perhaps we would be better in less crowded surroundings?'

'I think you are right,' said Holmes, leading the way. When we were seated in a quiet corner and had ordered coffee, Holmes went on, 'I think you know what this is about?'

Dawlish turned pale, and put a hand to

his head. 'That damned note, of course!'

'As you say. What was your intention?'

'I knew about the earlier notes, of course, my uncle had talked of them to me. I thought — well, I thought that I might jump on the bandwagon, as the saying is. Not that I could afford to buy shares in Forrage's myself, even at the lower price, but I knew my uncle would do so. I had hopes that, if he took the firm over, I would get a decent job as managing director or something of the kind.'

'And in due course inherit the shares?'

'Good Lord! I had no intention — Mr Holmes, you cannot think that I meant anything — Good Lord!' said Dawlish again, and turned very pale.

'No,' said Holmes slowly, 'I do not believe that you did. But your thoughtless action at Henley Grange, the interference with the fence, might have had disastrous, fatal, consequences. Mr Forrage might have been killed. Or even your uncle.'

'Good Lord!'

'Worse, Watson here might have been injured,' said Holmes sternly. 'And that would have been unforgivable.'

'Yes, indeed,' stammered Dawlish. 'Well, Mr Holmes, you need have no further fears. There will be no more tomfoolery, I promise you.'

'Very well,' said Holmes.

Dawlish stood up and held out his hand. Holmes smiled, shook the other's hand vigorously, and nodded a farewell as Dawlish made his way, somewhat unsteadily, to the door.

'And what of the shares bought by Sir Hubert?' I asked Holmes. 'You insisted that Forrage repay those whom he had defrauded, and Sir Hubert has, albeit unwittingly, also profited by all this.'

Holmes frowned. 'You say 'albeit unwittingly', and I think that is the significant point. The shares bought by Sir Hubert were legitimately bought,' he said. 'As Sir Hubert himself observed, there is a proverb about rats and sinking ships. Had the owners of those shares not lost faith in Forrage's — and in Sherlock Holmes! — they would not have sold. I think we had best say no more about that, and let Sir Hubert keep the shares he bought, as a reward for his confidence in the store's future.'

'That sounds fair.' I frowned. 'One last little point does still puzzle me, Holmes.'

'Only one?'

I ignored this. 'If — no, not 'if', but rather 'since' — since Forrage himself wrote the earlier notes, and did the damage, why on earth should he wish to consult you? After all, there was a possibility that you would uncover the truth.'

'Only a possibility?' said Holmes with a laugh.

'Go on, then, a probability! A certainty, if you insist. You did, when all is said and done, find out that it was Forrage. And even a less able investigator might have found out the truth. Why would Forrage consult anyone, least of all the world's best detective?'

Holmes smiled modestly, or as modestly as he was able, and said, 'Having started writing the notes, making the threats, he had to be seen to do something about it, Watson. He could not hope to let things go on without taking, or appearing to take, some action. Indeed, I myself noted the same point, and made some discreet enquiries at the weekend house party. I discovered that Sir Hubert had been the one who insisted on my being consulted — 'Might as well have the best, since we're paying anyway,' as he told me.'

'Sir Hubert? Another little puzzle there, Holmes, if Sir Hubert had been the writer of the latest note.'

He nodded agreement. 'As you say. I could explain why Forrage had called me in, he had no choice. But if Sir Hubert had been the second culprit, why, as you so perceptively ask, should he insist on my involvement. That is one of the things which made me wonder, the other being that Sir Hubert had quite openly bought Forrage's shares. Yet the latest note was indubitably written on a typewriter owned by Sir Hubert's firm!'

'All explained, though, now? Tell me, Holmes, what of young Herbert Dawlish? Think he will go straight from now on?'

'I imagine so,' said Holmes. 'He did not strike me as a hardened villain, merely rather misguided. I think he will be a model citizen from henceforth.'

'I wonder if old Forrage will do the same! Mind you, he will have to look out. His finances will take a savage beating,' I said. 'I shouldn't wonder if he has to sell Henley Grange, and perhaps even the shares he owned to begin with.'

Holmes shook his head. 'It would be no more than he deserves, I agree. But I fancy that he will rise, like a phoenix from the ashes.' He stood up and took his hat from the table. 'Are you ready, Watson?'

Epilogue

A Return to Forrage's

Holmes was right. As a result of his uncle's having a large shareholding in Forrage's, young Herbert Dawlish was appointed to the board, and he actually acquired a reputation for being somewhat conservative, if not downright fuddy-duddy, in his business dealings. Many years later, on his uncle's death, Herbert became chairman of Forrage's, and did a remarkable job as such. As for A. W. Forrage himself, he recovered from the little set-back very rapidly, and was spared for almost exactly twenty years. It was perhaps a month after the announcement of his death that Holmes and I again visited the big store in Holborn. Sherlock Holmes had been retired for many years, and it was on one of his rare visits to the metropolis that we found ourselves once more 'foraging around Forrage's'.

One could say that the store was not much changed, and in substance that would be true. It was those topicalities of theme and decor that had changed to suit the times. As we sat in the café where once we had heard a string trio we were now entertained by a quartet of Indian musicians with brass instruments. Will Goldston was no longer manager of the conjuring department, having departed to open his own magic store near Leicester Square. And in the basement, where the circus had been, a roller-skating rink now did a thriving trade.

Yet it was all still a part of Forrage's, where it is said to this day that one can buy anything from a thimble to an elephant!

We do hope that you have enjoyed reading this large print book.

Did you know that all of our titles are available for purchase?

We publish a wide range of high quality large print books including:
Romances, Mysteries, Classics General Fiction Non Fiction and Westerns

Special interest titles available in large print are:
The Little Oxford Dictionary Music Book, Song Book Hymn Book, Service Book

Also available from us courtesy of Oxford University Press:
Young Readers' Dictionary (large print edition) Young Readers' Thesaurus (large print edition)

For further information or a free brochure, please contact us at:
Ulverscroft Large Print Books Ltd., The Green, Bradgate Road, Anstey, Leicester, LE7 7FU, England.
Tel: (00 44) **0116 236 4325**
Fax: (00 44) **0116 234 0205**

Other titles in the
Linford Mystery Library:

THAT INFERNAL TRIANGLE

Mark Ashton

An aeroplane goes down in the notorious Bermuda Triangle and on board is an Englishman recently heavily insured. The suspicious insurance company calls in Dan Felsen, former RAF pilot turned private investigator. Dan soon runs into trouble, which makes him suspect the infernal triangle is being used as a front for a much more sinister reason for the disappearance. His search for clues leads him to the Bahamas, the Caribbean and into a hurricane before he resolves the mystery.

THE GUILTY WITNESSES

John Newton Chance

Jonathan Blake had become involved in finding out just who had stolen a precious statuette. A gang of amateurs had so clever a plot that they had attracted the attention of a group of international spies, who habitually used amateurs as guide dogs to secret places of treasure and other things. Then, of course, the amateurs were disposed of. Jonathan Blake found himself being shot at because the guide dogs had lost their way . . .

THIS SIDE OF HELL

Robert Charles

Corporal David Canning buried his best friend below the burning African sand. Then he was alone, with a bullet-sprayed ambulance containing five seriously injured men and one hysterical nurse in his care. He faced heat, dust, thirst and hunger; and somewhere in the area roamed almost two hundred blood-crazed tribesmen led by a white mercenary with his own desperate reasons for catching up with the sole survivors of the massacre. But Canning vowed that he would win through to safety.

HEAVY IRON

Basil Copper

In this action-packed adventure, Mike Faraday, the laconic L.A. private investigator, stumbles by accident into one of his most bizarre and lethal cases when he is asked to collect a fifty thousand dollar debt by wealthy club owner, Manny Richter. Instead, Mike becomes involved in a murderous web of death, crime and corruption until the solution is revealed in the most unexpected manner.

ICE IN THE SUN

Douglas Enefer

It seemed like the simplest of assignments when the Princess Petra di Maurentis flew into London from her island in the sun — but anything private eye Dale Shand takes on invariably turns out to be vastly different from what it seems. Like the alluring Princess herself, whose only character flaw is a tendency to steal anything not actually nailed to the floor. Dale is in it deep, mixed-up with the most colourful bunch of fakes even he has ever run up against . . .

THE DRUGS FARM

P. A. Foxall

The police suspect an American hard-line drugs dealer escaped from custody to be in England and they know of the expensively organised release from a maximum security prison of an industrial chemist. Their investigations are hampered by their sheer innocence of the criminals' resources and capacity for corruption, even in the citadel of power. No wonder there seems little chance of uncovering the criminals' product — a dangerous and hallucinogenic drug — that could threaten the young everywhere.